SIR, WHEN IS OUR NEXT STOP?

Sir, When Is Our Next Stop?

Terry G. Susong

To order additional copies of this book, contact:
Xlibris Corporation
1-888-795-4274
www.Xlibris.com
Orders@Xlibris.com
116282

Contents

DEDICATION

IN MEMORY OF MASTER SERGEANT

JAMES WILLIAM CLINE

AUGUST 3, 1936-MARCH 16, 2111

Thank you for hiring me. You made this book possible.

TAPS
DAY IS GONE . . . GONE THE SUN . . .
FROM THE LAKES . . . FROM THE HILLS . . .
FROM THE SKY . . .
ALL IS WELL . . . SAFELY REST . . .
GOD IS NIGH

ACKNOWLEDGEMENTS

A SPECIAL THANK YOU TO

My editor—Beverly "SilverBee" Scofield.
For stirring the bowl of alphabet soup I gave her and making it into a wonderful book.

My niece—Tammy Honesty
For drawing a map of my journeys and painting from it a great front cover.

My daughter and her husband—Teresa and Ray Miller
For all of their help and support.

My brother and sister-in-law—Dennie and Jill Susong
For the extraordinary support they gave to me.

My former pastor—Dennis Cagle
For his spiritual leadership and for writing the Pastor's Foreword.

My Vonore Baptist Church family
For their support and prayers.

My wife—Connie Elaine Fodrea Susong
For her prayers, for sometimes joining me on the road, but most of all
For being my steadfast and loving partner on the journey called Life.

Last, but foremost—My personal friend and Savior the Lord Jesus Christ
For showing His travel mercies in all the miles I drove without an accident.
And for letting me give the Christian message to so many young people.

PREFACE

This book grew into a full-fledged story while I was on a voyage of my own—traveling from Knoxville, Tennessee to Fort Knox Kentucky or Fort Jackson and Parris Island, South Carolina. In three-and-a-half years, I transported more than a thousand young men and women to their basic training stations. And during those three-and-a-half years, I have heard a thousand stories. I will be sharing many of these stories with you.

I served two years in the Army myself, half of that time spent as a medic in Vietnam. That was the experience helping to bridge the generation gap between the future soldiers and me.

During the six or eight hours I was with my troops, in a van we called *The Big Gray Ugly*, I had plenty of time to build a rapport with them before I turned them over to "the lions" (my term for the drill instructors who would turn them into our fighting men and women). At the end of each journey, I was able to give them a small cross pin, a *Psalm 91* book, and a prayer. I have many letters from my troops. These letters speak volumes to me of how this short van drive changed them. I will share with you not only some of these stories but also some of the actual letters and, in the process, you will learn how these young folks changed me.

I had no intentions of writing a book when I started the job, but after a few months had passed, I noticed that people were responding to the stories I told. They were paying close attention and asking to hear more. "Why don't you write a book?" they'd say. After hearing this for the tenth time (I am a little slow sometimes.), I said, "Okay, I'll write a book!"

It didn't start out as a spiritual book but just some yarns about fun things that happened on the way to basic training. But when I saw that lives were changing, the book transformed itself into an account of one man's mission to serve his Lord. How did I know my message was changing lives? The news reached me in letters, emails and even by telephone when one young man called me at home on his graduation day from basic training. He'd found my card in his wallet, with my telephone number printed on it, and wanted to thank me once again for taking him to Fort Jackson.

My hope is that this book will give you a laugh and maybe even bring a tear or two. My goal is for you to enjoy reading my book as much as I enjoyed writing it!

Terry G. Susong

PASTOR'S FOREWORD

When is our next stop? That's a fair question, but like many other questions in life, the answer may vary from one person to another. In a day when so many have adopted a mindset that nothing is absolute, Terry has asked a simple question that when truly considered, brings us back to that reality of yesteryear—a time when some things were of extreme importance while other things were just not worth getting riled up over.

As you probe the pages that lie before you, you will find one thing that truly matters—identity. Whether you've served in the armed forces or not, whether you were called upon without a choice or if you volunteered. You are sure to identify with the personalities and emotions found in the lives of the men and women you are about to meet.

You will be introduced to some by their real names, while others you will know only by an assigned name, like Rose for example. I personally have not met most of the characters within these fascinating pages, but the two main characters I have known quite well. The first is obviously the author, whose memory has amazed me and whose drive and passion for sharing this treasure with the world has challenged me. The second is the Savior who surely must have placed the desire for this book in the heart of a man. He's the same One who will, if you take it slow enough, give you the ability to identify with the characters—to laugh with them and weep with them, to actually feel like you yourself, climbed up in the "old gray ugly" and took that ride without knowing the answer to the infamous question, When is our next stop?"

None of us can know for sure when, but we can know where. My prayer today is that you meet all the characters and get to know them, especially the One who knows when.

Dennis Cagle M.TH
Sr. Pastor Vonore Baptist Church

INTRODUCTION

THE MAN WHO DRIVES THE VAN

My name is Terry G. Susong, and just so you'll know who is entrusted with the lives of so many of the recruits destined to travel from Knoxville, Tennessee, to their basic training stations, here is a little bit about me and my life up until now. I was born in Morristown, Tennessee where I lived with my mother, father, and little brother, Dennie. We moved to Middletown, Ohio after my first grade, and I finished elementary and high school there.

To give you an honest picture of my youthful character, I had a pet rabbit that we kept in the back yard in a cage. I decided to put my four-year-old brother in the rabbit cage and let the rabbit go. It seemed like a fun thing to do. When my mom asked where Dennie was, I said, "Oh, I put him in the rabbit cage." That was the first time I can remember getting into trouble. I had an old collie dog whose name was Trouble. *Come to think of it, maybe they named the dog after me.* The character trait must have stuck, too. The other day I was in church and when the preacher saw me coming toward him he said, "Here comes trouble!"

I was drafted into the Army in April of 1969. I was 19 years old, the same age as most of the recruits I took to their basic training. Here's how I came to be *The Man Who Drives the Van.*

When my wife, Connie, and I left Ohio and moved back to Tennessee, I went through a few jobs that I hated. For about a year, I worked in a mushroom factory in 36 degree inside temperatures and twelve-hour days. The pay was okay, though, and I got all the free mushrooms we could eat. I drove a forklift for a food warehouse company and hated that, too.

For a while, I had a fun job for the Cincinnati Reds working as an EMT in their Kid's Zone. I got to dress as a fan and wear a fanny pack with bandages and other cool stuff to treat the little darlings when they fell down and hurt their little pinkies—and other parts. I worked about fifty games a year and made a grand total of $50.00 a game. Since I was a big baseball fan, the money didn't matter all that much. The downside to it was that during that time the Reds had three of the worst seasons in their history.

Finally, I drove a pickup truck for a car dealership for over 400 miles a day, delivering new car parts in east Tennessee and southern Virginia. That was the job that led me to Executive Sedan and Limo, the company contracted to transport recruits. I was looking for a job to drive limos, so I looked them up in the yellow pages and talked to Tony, one of the owners of the company. He said they didn't need any drivers, but when he heard about my driving experience he suddenly discovered an opening. We agreed to a trial run of two trips, just to see if the job was a good fit.

Based in Knoxville, Tennessee, Executive Sedan made trips, always nonstop, to one or two of the destinations and back to Knoxville. Fort Jackson, South Carolina, was almost three hundred miles one way; and continuing on to Parris Island, North Carolina, meant another one hundred-forty miles; so, a round trip to Fort Jackson and Parris Island, then back to Knoxville, added up to over nine hundred miles driving in one day. Fort Knox, Kentucky, was a little less than three hundred miles one-way, which made it a six hundred mile day for the driver. I made these trips for three years, and along with firefighting in Middletown, it was one of the best jobs I ever had.

My first trip was to Parris Island. I sat in the passenger seat of the van we called *The Big Gray Ugly* and looked back at young men, all of them between the ages of eighteen and twenty-one, talking and laughing. The longer the trip, the more they talked. The more they talked, the more they grew to be friends. I took notes of landmarks and drew a map of the interstates as we traveled through Tennessee, North Carolina, and South Carolina.

The plan was for me to ride along that Monday and Wednesday. Then, if I liked the job, I would start making trips on my own. Three or four hours into the trip Tony's cell phone rang. After a brief conversation, he hung up, looked at me and said, "Well, how do you like the job so far?" I said, "So far I like it."

"Well, good. Wednesday you're on your own."

Sweat beads popped out on my forehead. *How I wished I had taken more detailed notes.* On the way home I got to drive *The Big Gray Ugly* for the first time. We had been traveling round trip without a stop. With my eyes burning and watering, I made it back to Knoxville the next morning. That trip turned out to be the first of several hundred.

I do believe that God put me in that position, at just that stage of my life. Some people say it turned into a ministry. I'd have to agree with them. During three years on the job, I met well over a thousand of our future service men and women. I asked them to call me Terry, but most of them ended up calling me sir.

At the end of each trip it was my privilege to say a prayer before I released them to the "lions." I always asked their permission. I never had anyone refuse my offer. I also gave them a card with my name, address, phone number and email address and, in the left upper corner an embossed golden cross with a reference to Psalm 91.

> *He that dwelleth in the secret place of the Most High*
> *Shall abide under the shadow of the Almighty.*

I've received letters from many of the soldiers after they got settled in basic training. They were a big part of my reward (and still are). When the first letter arrived, I cried like a baby. Now that I am used to the letters, I just read them several times—then say a prayer for the safety of the writers.

Now it is my privilege to share my experience with others. There is a lot to tell about the folks I call *My Troops* and who just call me *Sir*. I hope you'll enjoy the book. Come on board *The Big Gray Ugly* or *The Big Green Ugly*. I'll try to put a smile on your face or a tear in your eye. Either way we'll have fun! If you need a break let me know. Just say, "*Sir, when is our next stop?*"

CHAPTER 1

THE NIGHT BEFORE SHIPPING

T'was the night before shipping and all thru the house,
Not a recruit was stirring, not even a mouse.
Tucked up in their beds and barely alive, dreading that wake-up at 0445.
Hurry up, hurry up, get on your feet; not a moment to waste, just a quick bite to eat
It's 0545, so don't make a fuss; its 0545, time to get on the bus!
A quick ride to MEPS; we'll be there by 0630.
A full morning of testing—it's not gonna be purty.
You passed? It's a wonder! You're sure a sorry looking bunch.
But you're *my troops*, you've made it, and I've got a hunch
What's coming next will be full of surprise. So listen closely to what I advise
Right now I say hurry up, hurry up; here comes the van
That will take you to basic, and I am the man,
The man you'll depend on as a few hours go past,
Till I hand you all over to your keepers at last!
So hurry up, hurry up! Here comes the van.
You are *my troops*, and I am *the man!*

Yes, I was the man who drove the van. As it turns out, though, another man helped to ease the new recruits through their introduction into the military. His name was Ken and it was his job to process the recruits for their night's stay at the Crowne Plaza Hotel in downtown Knoxville. Some of them, I knew, would soon be my troops. I always asked the recruits what they thought of the hotel. Some of them might never have experienced such luxury, since descriptions of the room with so many big, fluffy pillows came up often, as well as the nice workout room.

The recruits talked a lot about the man who checked them into the hotel and briefed them. They described him as firm but caring. Over a period of time, the name of Ken kept coming up so often, I finally decided I had to meet this man who played such an important role for my troops.

One day I called the hotel and asked to speak to Ken. I introduced myself and we made an appointment to meet at the hotel the following day. I knew the location of the hotel because Connie and I once stayed there while visiting Knoxville, before we made the move from Ohio. Ken's office was on the second floor, and I reached it just at the appointed time. After our introductions, I sat down across from a gray haired man I guessed to be about my age. He gave me permission to audio tape our interview. For the next two hours we talked about our previous service in the Army. We had served in Vietnam during the same time period.

We were interrupted several times, as new people would enter the room for their interview with Ken. This was a chance to see him in action. Just as the recruits had told me, he was firm, all right, but funny, too. He gave the same speech to each one. Later Ken told me his speaking rate was one hundred seventy-nine words a minute. He explained that while most people easily comprehended eighty to one hundred words a minute, speaking fast forced them to listen more closely.

Ken gave each recruit a meal ticket for supper and breakfast. They were allowed free time and could go downtown or meet at the hotel with family members. Bed check was at eleven o'clock, and the dreaded wake-up call would come at 0445 hours. They had an hour and a half to get ready, eat breakfast and meet the shuttle that would take them to MEPS at 0615 hours. All this was preparation for the regimentation to come.

"Would you like a tour of our facility here?" I thought Ken would never ask! I was ready to see where my troops spent their night before shipping. As for them, they had their pick of lazing in the Crowne Plaza Hotel's indoor swimming pool, working out in the fitness center, roaming downtown places for eating or entertainment, or simply watching television in their plush rooms.

I left Ken knowing that my troops were in good hands and enjoying a great night before shipping out.

CHAPTER 2

MY TROOPS

My troops, as I've called the recruits on their way to basic training, came from every kind of cultural background. They never failed to interest and amaze me, and I'm happy to say their letters have shown they held me in high regard, as well. They were on their way into the unknown, some afraid, others stoic, but all in need of a source of strength for what was to come. It was my good fortune to be there for them, to be the man they called *Sir*.

It helped us to feel comfortable together during the long drives to exchange stories, both personal and anecdotal, and always they came up with questions? "Sir, when is our next stop?" *When is our next stop! We hadn't even left the building yet!* My goal each time I pulled out of MEPS was to give each person as much freedom as possible on their last day of freedom. I had very few problems with these recruits. They had been cooped up in a building at the Military Entrance Processing Station (MEPS) for close to seven hours, with "hurry up and wait" orders. When I'd arrive at one o'clock, even though they didn't know me, they would greet me joyfully, for I was their ticket out of there. Yet, they were already wondering where and when we'd be stopping next!

Once we were on the way and conversation began, they'd almost always ask, "*Sir*, did you serve in the military?" Of course my answer was (with a big smile on my face), "Yes." They'd want to know what branch, so I'd have a chance to talk about being in the Army. I liked to think those talks relieved some of the stress for them. "I served two years in the Army as a combat medic and one year of it was in Vietnam." And I'd tell them I was drafted. This always got a mix of reactions. Some of the recruits would remain silent. Sometimes I'd hear, "My dad served in Vietnam," or "My grandfather served in Vietnam!" Wow did that make me feel old.

On one trip to Parris Island, I had a full load of a dozen or so "wannabe" Marines in the *The Big Grey Ugly* with a young woman riding up front with me. She was only seventeen and her father had been required to sign before she could join. A couple of hours into the trip, while everyone was laughing and having a good time, the questions began. "*Sir*, did you serve in the military?" And, "What branch?" This time there was another one, "Did you go to war?" Just as I opened my mouth to say, "Vietnam," My front-seat passenger spoke up with, "Oh, World War Two?" That brought a roar of laughter so loud I could almost feel the van starting to rock side to side! Above all the laughter I could just barely hear a squeaky little voice saying, "I'm sorry, Sir. I'm sorry. I don't know my wars." She and I become the butt of many jokes for the remainder of the trip.

Another time, on a trip to Fort Knox, the recruit who was riding shotgun told about his stepfather's service in Vietnam. He was obviously proud of the man's toughness. He told story after story about the heroics he'd performed. From the back seat one of the recruits asked the big question, "*Sir*, did you serve in Vietnam?" When I said, "Yes, I served one year," the young man turned around and addressed the small group in the back seat and said very loudly: "Guys, don't mess with this man. He will kick your ***. It was a guarantee I wouldn't have *any* problems with that group!

Eventually there was one question I always asked of them, "Why did you join?" The stories they told were not always happy one, but there was generally hope that things would be better in the future. As the questions arose, the recruits and I began to tell our stories, and we became a close band of travelers. I was their *Sir* and they were *My Troops*.

CHAPTER 3

PSALM 91

I was searching for a Bible verse to place on my business cards, and after looking through several verses, chapters and books of the Bible I stopped at the *Book of Psalms, Psalm 91*. It was exactly right—and not just a verse, a whole chapter!

The Bible says, "Seek and you shall find," and there it was. *Psalm 91* would give my troops the comfort they needed in a time of unusual stress. And my card, with its cross in the corner and the words of *Psalm 91*, would point the way for them to find it.

I didn't think I would ever get to know what impact my little two by four card would have on the future of these soldiers, but I would pray for them and give them the card. Most of them thanked me. Many of them would promise to write. The reality is that I'd only get three or four letters a month, though I'd have loved to get that many every week. When one brought a tear to my eye, Connie would say, "You got a good one today, huh?" Yes, but every letter was precious.

I pray for all of my troops every night before I go to sleep, with a special prayer for each letter I receive. Most of these young men and women hurt physically and emotionally. I was blessed to be able to play a small, but I hoped significant, part in their lives. They took the time out of their busy lives to write a letter to a man they hardly knew. Something happened in those few hours that inspired them to write these letters, and I would cherish their letters for the rest of my life because they inspired me, as well.

Thank you, God, not only for the blessing that You have given me, but also the blessing that You have passed on to these young people through me.

I should add the disclaimer that I don't have written permission to quote from Psalm 91. However, I'm not worried because the Author of the entire Bible is a personal friend of mine. I have known Him all my life, and He has been by my side all the way! In high school, through those tests, without Him I wouldn't have received that C+! At the firehouse when the fire alarm went off, He was there riding beside me on the fire truck. And as I drove the troops to their basic training, I always felt His presence.

There was a dual purpose to my advice to go to chapel every Sunday morning. Besides the spiritual benefit, it's the only place to get away from the drill sergeant! Then, of course, the chaplain just might find something of interest to say.

Just before I dropped my troops off at their destination, we always had a meal at Shoney's. After we finished eating, we'd move out to the parking lot and while they policed the van to get rid the accumulated trash, I'd start putting together the little packet of goodies for them. I gave them my card, a little lapel cross, and a copy of *Psalm 91: God's Shield of Protection*, written by Peggy Joyce Ruth and Angelia Ruth Schum. A Google search had told me how, since World War I, *Psalm 91* has been called *The Soldiers Prayer*, so I thought they could really use it. But I also asked them to pass it along to someone else if they didn't think they would read it.

PSALM 91

KING JAMES VERSION

1   —He that dwelleth in the secret place of the most High shall abide under the shadow of the Almighty.
2   I will say of the Lord, He is my refuge and my fortress: my God; in him will I trust.
3   Surely he shall deliver thee from the snare of the fowler, and from the noisome pestilence.
4   He shall cover thee with his feathers, and under his wings shalt thou trust: his truth shall be thy shield and buckler.

5 Thou shalt not be afraid for the terror by night; nor for the arrow that flieth by day;

6 Nor for the pestilence that walketh in darkness; nor for the destruction that wasteth at noonday.

7 A thousand shall fall at thy side, and ten thousand at thy right hand; but it shall not come nigh thee.

8 Only with thine eyes shalt thou behold and see the reward of the wicked.

9 Because thou hast made the Lord, which is my refuge, even the most High, thy habitation;

10 There shall no evil befall thee, neither shall any plague come nigh thy dwelling.

11 For he shall give his angels charge over thee, to keep thee in all thy ways.

12 They shall bear thee up in their hands, lest thou dash thy foot against a stone.

13 Thou shalt tread upon the lion and adder: the young lion and the dragon shalt thou trample under feet.

14 Because he hath set his love upon me, therefore will I deliver him: I will set him on high, because he hath known my name.

15 He shall call upon me, and I will answer him: I will be with him in trouble; I will deliver him, and honour him.

16 With long life will I satisfy him, and shew him my salvation.

CHAPTER 4

SIR, DID YOU SERVE?

The question, "Sir, did you serve?" inevitably came up. It gave me a chance to get on the same footing as the recruits, to let them know I understood what they were going through. The question always took me right back to my first day in the Army.

No one, in the service, now or in the past, could possibly forget that first day. Mine was not a pretty sight. It began in the early hours of the day when the bus left Middletown for the thirty-two minute drive to Cincinnati, Ohio. When I arrived there, I had to walk around for most of the day in my underwear, following "hurry up and wait" orders. Finally, the welcome order came, "Get your pants on, soldier; you're going to Fort Dix, New Jersey."

I had my first airplane flight that day, which turned into a long day, because we didn't land in Pittsburgh, Pennsylvania until midnight. Just like in the movies, there was another big bus waiting to take us on a two-hour ride to Fort Dix. After being up all day and night, I had no trouble falling asleep on the ride.

The next thing I heard was the sound of the air brakes and the bus rolling to a stop. The door opened and a man wearing a large, round, green hat entered. At the top of his voice he yelled, "Welcome to Fort Dix! Now, *get off my bus*!" Some things never change. Seems like I had seen the movie—and I never did like the ending!

I was asked quite often if I enjoyed being in the Army. They would seem surprised when I gave them my truthful answer, an emphatic, "No!" Of course they wanted to know why not. I'd tell them that, unlike them, I was drafted. After my two years of service in the Army were over, I received an Honorable Discharge and went happily back to civilian life. I did tell them if I hadn't landed my career job as a full time firefighter, I would have gone back into the Army as Chaplain's Assistant. And I always told them of my pride in having served our country and how it continued to be important to try to be the first one to stand and salute Old Glory when it came by at special events.

I never went to college. Going into the Army was my first time so far away from home. Later on, when I went to Vietnam, I found out what far away from home really meant. Nothing hurts worse than being far away from home and loved ones for the first time and having a good old dose of homesickness.

One day, long after my own stretch in the Army, letters would come from some of my troops telling me how hard it was to be away from wives, kids, girlfriends or boyfriends, and moms and dads. Reading their words would give me that old gut feeling, all over again. I wanted to tell them they'd learn that the aches and pains from marching all day or running five miles would feel better after a hot shower and eight hours of sleep, but I knew the only thing that that would help the homesickness was the picture in the wallet or the rare call home.

Mail call could make or break a day. Seeing all the happy faces of those who were tearing open envelopes was painful if you name hadn't been called. Then again, no feeling in the world could beat getting a letter from home—even if, sometimes, the letter was from the old guy who drove you to basic training.

As for the letters I receive from my troops, they just keep coming. Sometimes there'd be a short dry spell and I would think maybe the letters had run dry. Eventually, though, they'd begin again, maybe when a new group reached a certain realization along the way and wanted to let me know they just *got* it. I'd be like a kid at Christmas opening up that metal mailbox to find a letter from one of my troops, but I'll continue praying for them, even if I never receive another letter.

I got an indescribable feeling whenever I prayed for those young men and women, as though the Holy Spirit was present. Of course, some of them bowed their heads just because I asked them to, but all of them bowed their heads in respect to God. The one thing their letters almost always mentioned was the prayer and how much they appreciated it.

During those years, I was trying to cover all the bases. It was my job to deliver these young people to their basic training destination safely. But I took it as my mission to give them as much spiritual encouragement as possible in our few hours on the road. By giving them the card with my mailing address, the book *Psalm 91* and the lapel pin, and saying a prayer for their safety, I could say goodbye to my troops with a clear heart.

"Sir, did you serve?" *What a question. I am still serving in the Army today—Gods' Army!*

CHAPTER 5

WHY DID YOU JOIN?

Just as the recruits asked, "Sir did you serve in the military?" I always tried to ask each one, "Why did you join the military?" There were a variety of predictable answers, although I saw a difference between the answers from the Army and Marines recruits.

Army

There were many more Army recruits on their way to basic training than future Marines. It really tore at my heart to listen to some of the reasons they joined the military. The number one answer was, "I was in a series of dead end jobs. I got tired of flipping hamburgers for a living." Most of them were between the ages of eighteen and twenty-two, sometimes newlywed with a baby due in a couple of months; or they would be getting married as soon as they got back from basic training. Although, over time I got used to the shocking answers, I never got over the sorrow they created.

A lot of their answers were about family respect. "Everyone in my family has been in the military for generations. My dad [or sometimes mother], my papaw, and all of my brothers have been in the military." Or, "No one in my family has been in the military, and I want to be the one to start the trend."

Because of the downturn in the economy, money was a big reason for joining up. "I received a $20,000 bonus for signing up as a transportation specialist [a truck driver]" or, "I received a $2,000 bonus for signing up my best friend." And, "I got married last Saturday so my wife will receive a check for a monthly housing allowance." Here's a tearjerker: "I've been homeless and living on the street for the last four months." I actually heard this more than once.

Education was also one of the main reasons for joining the Army. Joining the National Guard meant college tuition would be paid, as well as a monthly paycheck for living expenses. Those who already had some college years could use the education benefit to get an advanced degree. Those interested in becoming an officer, and who qualified, could go to Officer Candidate School (OCS) for four years. These were powerful incentives for recruits.

Occasionally, a few would turn up who had prior service and were re-entering the military. The reasons they gave were the same as the reasons given by the newly enlisted soldiers. I took one young man to Fort Jackson who had served five years in the Army. He'd been out of the Army for about a year when he finally realized he wasn't going to find a job. Needing to take care of his family, he came back to see his Uncle Sam. He was going to Fort Jackson not for basic training but for orientation and a new duty station. Since he was the only one I was transporting that time, we had a good conversation.

He told me about his previous years of service as one of the guards assigned to Arlington National Cemetery. He did most of the talking and I did most of the listening—for a change. As he was one of the soldiers who guarded the Tomb of the Unknown Soldier, he was often on national television—and, he said he had the videos to prove it. He talked about the different events he had participated in, some that drew national attention. He was a guard for the funeral of former President Ronald Reagan.

He went into great detail about the training he had to go through—a lot of spit and polish, as they say in the Army. He told me of the extensive background security check the government put him through. Listening to his stories made this one of the quickest trips I ever made to Fort Jackson.

With the Army in my past and in my roots, yet I could see a noticeable difference between Army and Marine recruitment standards. Although not all by any means, but some of these young men and women needed a second chance at life. I was glad the Army would bend over backwards and sometimes push the envelope to allow someone entry. No high school diploma? No problem! Not only would the Army take them in but it also made sure they received the proper schooling in order to qualify for a General Education Degree [GED] before going to basic training. Once sworn in, of course, the Army owned them, hearts and souls, to either make or break!

I heard someone say on a talk show one day that since we now have an all-volunteer Army, all we were getting as recruits were "bottom feeders and trailer trash." What a strong and ugly statement that is! Speaking from firsthand experience I beg to disagree. I've seen more upfront pride and determination from folks down on their luck than from recruits with a higher education and money in the bank.

I take many recruits to basic training whose lives have been turned upside down. Sometimes it looks as though they're to blame. They *allowed* themselves to get into drugs and alcohol. Most of the time I find out it was a product of how they were brought up. As they told me their stories, it became clear to me that one or both of the parents had a hand it. There were even times when both parents were in prison or had been at some time. This is where grandma often came into play to take care of the children. Thank God for grandmothers!

I heard a lot of moonshine stories and got quite an education on the "mountain dew" of the hills of Tennessee and North Carolina. A young man named Dewayne told me, "Grandpa gave me my first drink of moonshine when I was only eight years old." Whenever the subject of moonshine came up I always mentioned the name of Popcorn Sutton. Almost everyone knew him. One recruit even said, "Oh, that's my Dad's cousin!" Another one said, "I never met him but I have had some of his moonshine. *Um mm*! The best I ever had!"

The young folks I carried weren't moonshiners, and they might never have been in trouble with the law, but they poured out details of their lives that needed healing. It became my mission to help, as much as I could in the short time they were in my hands. Already, they were unrecognizable when they returned after twelve weeks in basic training. With God's help, the letters that came long after they'd left me provided an opportunity for me to continue ministering to these young folks.

I recently received a letter from a soldier named Victoria who said she was having problems with her marriage. She said she had started going to chapel. When I took her to Fort Jackson six weeks ago, our conversation was about going to chapel each Sunday. She said she used to be closer to God but that it was okay. I wrote her back and told her it was *not* okay and that she needed God more in her life than ever before, that she needed to have a daily prayer life and to start reading her Bible, too. I said I'd send her a Bible if she didn't have one. I prayed to God I wasn't coming on too strong—to her or any of my troops. The last thing I wanted was to drive them away from God. After we had written several letters back and forth,

Victoria let me know that things were getting better with her husband. She said she couldn't wait to get back home and patch things up with him.

One of the stories I told the recruits was about my first day in the Army. I hoped they'd not make the same mistake that I made. The entire day was a disaster I created all by myself. I've always been one to say the wrong thing at the wrong time just to get a laugh! Connie has nicknamed me Silver Tongue Susong! My first day in the Army was no exception. Whatever I said to the drill sergeant has been blotted out of my memory by the punishment it earned me.

It happened while were standing in formation. At the time I didn't even know what a formation was, but that was when my "silver tongue" kicked in, and when I came to the full attention of the drill sergeant. He pulled me off to the side and handed me over to one of his subordinates. I was escorted to the mess hall for twenty-four hours of KP duty.

I didn't know that the mess hall was the kitchen, nor did I know that KP actually stood for kitchen patrol. The mess hall was huge with a full-size kitchen in the middle. On each side of the kitchen was a large dining room with seating for hundreds of people. I soon learned everything I ever wanted to know about a mess hall and twenty-four hour KP duty.

Among the lessons I learned were how to peel potatoes the Army way, the way to serve the troops food, and how to wash dishes and clean out grease traps. I worked hard all day and all night. About four o'clock the next morning, I got so sleepy I went into the restroom, which I found out later was called a latrine. I sat down on the toilet and fell instantly sound asleep.

I don't how long I slept, but all of a sudden the stall door flew open and the cook yelled, ""What the hell are you doing in here?" I rubbed my eyes and said, "I'm going to the restroom!"

"Next time take your pants down! Now get back to work!"

After performing twenty-four hours of kitchen patrol, I thought the punishment was complete, but then I was ordered to see the commander of basic training. This did not make me happy. I entered the room and saw a large black officer with captain's bars on his shoulders. I gave him a shaky salute and said, "Private Susong, reporting, sir!"

The captain looked at me and said, "Soldier, how many grandmothers do you have?"

"Sir, I have two grandmothers!"

Without a second's hesitation he said "Well, you only have one now. One died, so pack your bags and go on back home!"

Of course I was shocked. What a way to tell anyone that they just lost a loved one! So, my second day in the Army I was headed back home for the funeral of the grandmother I had just kissed goodbye a week ago.

After the funeral, I returned to Fort Dix and had to start all over again. Things went well for the next ten weeks. Four days before graduation from basic training, I was told to go see the old man again. That was the nickname given to the officer in charge. Again, I knocked on the commander's door and was invited in. I saw it was the same officer I had talked to just a short ten weeks ago. I didn't know why I was in his office, with only four days to go until graduation. To my knowledge, I had kept my nose clean.

The commander addressed me with a familiar phrase, "Soldier, how many grandmothers do you have?" "*Was this a joke?* But I replied, "Sir, you know I was in here ten weeks ago, and you told me I only had one grandmother."

Then, without even a smile, he said, "Well, the other one died now. Pack your bags. You're going home." Here we go again. The end of my basic training is the same as my beginning. Now, I had another funeral to go to and my time as a soldier would be spent without even one grandmother back home praying for me.

Even though I didn't get to physically attend my graduation, I was allowed to graduate and go on to my new training site at Fort Sam Houston, Texas. I was even *allowed* to spend some time in Vietnam in 1969-1970.

My AIT (Advance Infantry Training) at Fort Sam Houston consisted of twelve, long weeks of Texas heat and humidity where I learned my skills as an Army Combat Medic. At the end of the training, I received orders for a place much hotter that Texas—Vietnam.

I landed at Saigon Airport in one hundred twenty degree heat—in the shade, if you could find any shade. It was one long year in Vietnam, but it was finally over and I was on the flight home. The flight attendant set a glass of champagne in front of me. "No thank you," I told her. "I don't drink."

She indicated a woman three rows back and said, "The nice lady back there bought it for you." I turned around and saw the sweetest smile from an elderly woman. I lifted the glass to my lips and gave her a little wink. I drank the glass of champagne in the honor of the little old lady who was honoring me as a soldier.

When I left Vietnam, I had five months left in the Army and could choose my next station. I chose Fort Knox, Kentucky because that was the closest base to home. My wife and I found a cute little house, right outside the base. One day, while standing outside in the driveway, I thought I saw someone I knew. I approached the large black man with captain's bars on his shoulders and said, "Sir, you look familiar!"

He greeted me with a smile and a handshake." You look familiar, too, soldier. Where have you been stationed?" I told him I'd just returned from Vietnam, but I had completed my AIT at Fort Sam Houston, Texas."

"Where did you take your basic?" he asked. I answered, "Fort Dix, New Jersey, sir."

"I was the basic training commander at Fort Dix for over a year." he said.

Then I told him the story about both my grandmothers dying. I asked him if he remembered me.

"Yes I do remember you!" Not a word of apology or explanation. We laughed and shook hands. I said, "Well, I don't have any grandmothers left. They all died last year."

Marines

Looking For A Few Good Men was the recruiting slogan for the Marines for many years. When I asked the future Marines, "Why did you join the Marines?" I'd get a different type answer than those from the Army recruits.

The number one answer was, "To serve my country, sir!" I'd also get the answer, "I want to be the best!" I'd also hear, "For God and country." A young man named Cody told me, "I want the best training I can get!" Since the Marines didn't give out bonus money to enlist, money was not an incentive.

One surprising answer that I got was, "I can't wait until I can put on my blues [the fancy uniform they would wear for graduation] and walk across that field in front of my family!"

Yes, the Marine "wannabes" were different. When at MEPS, I could pick them out of a crowd. Most of them had already conformed to the Marine way. They'd have short haircuts, be nicely dressed and clean cut.

The ride to Parris Island was always a fun time. There was a lot of laughter and bonding. They embraced me with respect. As time went on and the miles added up, we'd all get to know each other. The Marine guys and gals got very little sleep while on the trip. They were usually too wound up and excited!

Sometimes they would tell me things they wouldn't tell their best friends. One said, "I can tell you this because I'll never see you again!" One person told me a story about himself he had never told another soul. I could see the relief on his face that he was glad to be able to get it off his chest. If they asked me not to reveal in my book any of the details they told me I've always honored that request.

At times I feel like a bartender. Once I get these folks at ease with me and they trust me, the words just start to flow. One young man told me a story about his past that only his family and his therapist knew about, and now I know, but I won't go against my promises to my troops.

God bless our troops!

CHAPTER 6

FORT KNOX, KENTUCKY

After a while, my own military past became entwined with the many stories coming from the recruits in the back seats of the van. Memories came back of my last five months in the Army, which I spent at Fort Knox, Kentucky. From my short stay at Fort Knox, I didn't have many good memories. One good memory, though, was the birth of my daughter, Teresa. Years later, driving through the base, I could point out different landmarks to my troops. "And the big tall gray building on the right is the hospital where my daughter was born! Yesterday was her 40th birthday!" I would say with pride. "If you are doing the math, that was 1971." I guess that proved I was the old man they thought I was.

A lot had changed in forty plus years. Only a few of the old buildings were still standing and many of them had been abandoned or replaced by new buildings. One of the new buildings was a Burger King, with a small indoor playground for the younger kids. It was highly visible from the road. I would point out the playground and say, "See the playground inside Burger King? If you fail your obstacle course they'll bring you down here and make you practice on the playground!" By then most of my troops had become wise to my sense of humor. However some could still be fooled. "Are you serious?" I would look at them with a sheepish smile and they'd usually catch on. But even then, a few were still naive enough to think that I meant it.

Fort Knox was three hundred miles from Knoxville. Leaving at 1:00 p.m. would get us there about 7:00 or 7:30 p.m. We would always eat our last-stop meal at Cracker Barrel where we could play a game of checkers or wrack our brains with the little triangle pegboards they left on every table. In the winter, getting a seat in front of the wood-burning fireplace was a great boon.

After our meal we had about seventy miles to go. Back on Interstate 64, miles of orange barrels often promised road construction and maybe a late arrival. There were questions from some, while others would sink into silence. Always, though, they made a lot of cell phone calls.

As we approached the last seven miles point, I'd always stop at the Marathon gas station where the troops had a chance to smoke that last cigarette or take a last pinch of dip. Sometimes all the cigarettes had been smoked, as they hadn't known they had this last opportunity. In that case, I would send them inside to see Vicki behind the counter. She loved the troops and freely gave each of them a cigarette when they asked for it—but not dip!

As we approached the security gate at Knox, each recruit had to produce a photo picture ID to get past the uniformed guard. Both Fort Knox and Fort Jackson used uniformed police rather than military police to guard all the gates. Parris Island seemed to be the only one still using military police as gate guards.

On one of the trips to Fort Knox, I drove an unmarked vehicle, rather than the one marked prominently with the company logo. Used to driving right through, I was so busy talking to my troops I didn't realize I was at the wrong gate. When I pulled up to the gate, the guard greeted me and asked where I was going on base. At that instant it hit me that in the unmarked vehicle I should have gone to the main gate.

There were two guards at the gate, and one of them recognized me from a previous trip. Much taller than the other guard, he positioned himself so he could see over his partner's shoulder. I offered my explanation and the first guard asked, "Oh, you're here to play racquetball today, are you?" The taller guard moved his head up and down to signal that my answer should be yes, and I obeyed. After dutifully checking each ID, they smiled and waved us on. Maybe the password of day was racquetball! Maybe that was a seasonal password. In the spring the word might be baseball, and in the fall, football! It would be very interesting to find out if Homeland Security gave out such passwords.

CHAPTER 7

PARRIS ISLAND, SOUTH CAROLINA

Get your heads up and say, 'Aye, aye, sir!' These were the first words my troops heard when they arrived at Parris Island. The van door opened and the officer would be their "best friend" for the next thirteen weeks, continued to bark orders. *I said say, 'Aye, aye, sir!'* The recruits, young men and women, lifted their heads, looked straight ahead and screamed in their loudest voices, *"Aye, aye, sir!"*

"When I tell you to get out of this van, I want you to get everything you came here with and get on my yellow footprints. Do you understand? Say, 'Aye, aye, sir!'

Already learning the first lesson of basic training, the recruits let out an ear bursting, "Aye, aye, sir!" Then, without missing a beat, the DI wrapped up the introduction to Parris Island with another loud command: "Get out of this van, *NOW!*"

Next, all I could see was arms, legs, and feet trying to get out of the van. They couldn't have moved any faster if the van had been on fire! After all of the future soldiers were standing erect on the yellow foot prints, the DI returned to my van to close the side door. He placed his head inside the van and said, in a normal, friendly voice and with a smile, said, "You have a safe drive home!"

As I drove away I could hear his voice become robotic, delivering a message repeated many times over the years, "Welcome to Parris Island, South Carolina, home of The United States Marine Corps." From a block away, I could still hear, "Sir! Yes, sir!" The eight-hour journey with my troops had ended, but their adventure of a lifetime was just beginning—and their first steps were yellow ones.

John 3:16

On another trip to Parris Island, with a stop planned at Fort Jackson to drop off a couple of Army recruits, everyone had fallen asleep. Steve was riding up front with me and after a while he woke up and began to talk about his life. We had a long discussion about how he was brought up, and I started talking to him about Jesus. He listened with interest, and our talk went on for about forty-five minutes, then we were quiet for a while.

I was driving behind a big semi with a sign on back that read John 3:16. I broke the silence and said aloud, "John 3:16." Jon, who sat in the passenger seat directly behind me, said, "What did you say?" I repeated, "John 3:16. It's on the back of the truck." Jon started to laugh. "Do you want to hear something funny?" he said "My name is Jon—J.O.N—and my birthday is 3/16!"

We arrived at Fort Jackson and I pulled off into my prayer corner. Before I asked the recruits if they minded if I prayed for them, Jon put his hand on my shoulder and asked, "Sir, do you mind if I lead us in prayer?"

This was a first. I said, "As long as there is no objection from anyone, it'll be great." Everyone agreed they would be happy for Jon to pray for us. We all bowed our heads and Jon said the prayer. He prayed from his heart and it was beautiful. I could hear the passion in his voice as he prayed for the young men leaving the van at Fort Jackson and for our safe trip on to Parris Island.

Fort Jackson was to be the basic training station for all the recruits except Jon. I delivered them to the reception center, and Jon and I got back on the road. He started the conversation and told me he felt the call from God to be a minister. We talked for a long time about his future in the Marines. I told him he would be a great witness for Christ.

We arrived at Parris Island right on time. Once inside, I pulled over to the side of the road to pray for Jon 3/16. Once again he surprised me by asked me if he could say a prayer for me. The young man poured his heart out in his prayer to our Lord. After he finished the prayer, I said one for him. It was a truly special time for me. Jon promised I would be one of the first people he writes to.

Two weeks passed and I had not yet heard from Jon. Then one day, shuffling through the electric and water bills I found a small envelope with Jon 3:16 in the return address. Jon had kept his word and written to the old man who drove him to basic training.

"Sir, Get Back In Your Car, Now!"

Five miles from the front gate of Parris Island I would always begin to give my troops a final heads up. On one trip I had two anxious young "wannabe" Marines, so when I started with the run down, they listened attentively to every word. "One of three things will happen when we get to the gate. Number one, the MP's will take our driver licenses, look at them and just wave us though. Number two, they will look in the car and play some word games with you. Maybe they'll yell at you and make you put your heads down on your laps. Okay, number three is the worst case scenario, they'll tell us to pull over to the side and they'll yell at you some more. And they will also give you a lecture on running away from the Island."

I have been pulled to the side only a couple of times in the hundreds of trips through the Parris Island gates. This time, I was driving a rental car, which was usually not a problem, so I wasn't worried. As I drove up to the gate, an MP came out of the guard shack. I rolled down the window and handed him the driver's licenses of the two recruits. The MP asked where I was going on the Island. I told him I had two new people, and I was going to the receiving area. He asked for identification for me and for my company. If I had been driving *The Big Green Ugly,* the proper identification would have been printed on the side of the van.

I have been through the gate in a rental car many times with no problem. Without cracking a smile the MP ordered me to pull over to the side. I thought *this is going to be that worst scenario I warned my troops about.* Little did I know this would be the worst scenario I had *ever* encountered at Parris Island.

I had to wait for approximately ten minutes. In the meantime, I used my cell phone to call Wilma and report that I was having a difficult time getting through the gate at PI. I also wanted her to know an MP would be calling her soon.

When the MP returned, I rolled down the window and asked, "What seems to be the problem?" He said, "Sir, because you're driving a rental car, we must check you out thoroughly, to make sure you are who you say you are. For all we know, you could be the father of these two young men and just trying to sneak on base."

Then he asked for the packets of the two young men, which included all of their official paperwork, and went back into his little shack. In a few moments, another MP drove up in a police car. Now I had two MPs to deal with. Another fifteen minutes passed by in silence. I saw a movement in the rearview mirror and saw two more MPs standing twenty feet behind my car.

Suddenly, a pain started in my left leg—a Charlie horse I'd experienced many times before, so I knew the only way to relieve it would be to get out of the car and stretch my leg. I opened the door and stepped out. That was when I heard a stentorian voice say, "*Sir, get back in the car, NOW!*" It sounded like a scene from the television series, "*Cops!*" But by that time I was out of the car.

I could see the two MPs standing with their hands on their pistols. I answered with the same intensity they'd had in their voices. "*That,*" I said, "*will not be possible.* I have a Charlie horse in my leg, and I cannot do it!" I grabbed my left upper leg and limped away from them in pain.

Finally back in the car and free from pain, I sat with the recruits and we waited. At length, the first MP returned and said, "Well, sir, you are who you say you are. I will follow you to your destination at which time I'll return your license." He handed the packets and licenses back to the recruits and the rest went off without a hitch.

It takes a lot to get me upset, but I *was* upset. In the three years I'd been transporting recruits, I had never been treated the way I was that evening. After delivering my two young men, I heard a rap on my side window. I rolled it down and the MP handed in my driver's license. He said, "Have a nice night!"

I called Wilma to vent about what had happened. She understood fully my feelings. Being a Marine Corps wife for more than thirty years, she knew how things could change with the security of the base.

Some time later, on another trip in a rental car, my cell phone rang as I neared Parris Island. It was Wilma who said she had contacted the Drill Instructor in charge and she gave me his telephone number. I drove up to the guard shack, and the same MP from the previous trip stepped outside his guard shack just as the rental car came to a stop.

"Good evening, sir. May I see your identifications?" He said it in his trained MP voice, and it was not accompanied by a smile. "Where are you headed tonight?"

I handed him the driver's licenses. "I'm taking this young man to the reception center." Then I asked, "Do you remember me from a couple of weeks ago?" Because of his slight build, the Marine had no trouble looking directly in my eyes. He gave me a big smile and said, "Oh, you're the guy with the Charlie horse!" We both had a good laugh and he let me pass with no problems.

I am an Army man from my roots. However, I do enjoy transporting my Marine troops, but they are definitely a different bunch of young men and women.

CHAPTER 8

THE LONG RIDE HOME

I looked at the clock on the dashboard radio and it read 10:30 p.m. It had taken eight hours and more than four hundred miles to deliver that day's recruits to Parris Island—cargo I considered precious.

After a half-day of work, I was alone with my radio, my cell phone, and the Lord (not necessarily in that order of importance). I was just leaving Parris Island when I picked up my cell phone to call Wilma and report I was homeward bound. This would only take a couple of minutes unless one of us was in a talkative mood or something of importance had happened since our last conversation a few hours ago. She might give me an updated weather report about rain, snow or some obstacle on the road ahead of me.

The next cell phone call went to Connie, and I listened to her tell about her day at work. She had taken on a job at the local food market and always had a story or two to share. After a few minutes she asked me what kind of group I had tonight, and it went on from there. We're both happy to hear the other's voice, and we filled up an hour or so of conversation. Eventually, one of us found a way to shut down for the night. Connie needed to get to bed for an early morning wakeup.

My night was almost over and my early morning had just begun. I turned to my favorite past time—listening to the radio. I hit seek button more times than I can count over the next several hours. It made me think of my younger days when the radio had only two knobs to turn. At the end of the dial, there was only one direction to turn the knob—back the opposite way, listening to the same radio stations. FM radio hadn't been invented yet, so the choices were one staticky station or another.

My choice of radio stations included oldies (1960's and early 1970's); talk radio (Coast-to-Coast, unless they started talking about ghosts or UFOs); Sean Hannity or Herman Cain; or country (unless I had just listened to eight hours of it earlier in the day). No rap or heavy metal music would enter my ears for more than a second or two. (I knew where to find the seek button!) And finally, I liked to listen to Dr. Charles Stanley preach the word or, occasionally, other Bible teaching preachers.

For my first year and a half at this job, every Monday night and Tuesday morning I spent driving to and from Parris Island. Sometimes a Fort Jackson stop would be piggybacked on the trip. My troops sometimes asked if I got lonely on the long ride home. My answer is no, although I did get mighty tired.

A year after I began to drive for Executive Sedan and Limo, a government inspector randomly checked my records and discovered that I was driving sixteen hours without a break. I was already maintaining a log like the ones kept by eighteen-wheeler jockeys. Now I would have to follow the regulations about stopping to rest. The sixteen-hour round trips without sleep became twenty-four hour journeys. Two hours after leaving Parris Island there was, yes, another Pilot gas station. It had a McDonald's next door, so I felt safe sleeping—or trying to sleep—because the place was well lit and people came and went in the parking lot all night long. I'd be back on the road after four or five hours, with seven hours and three hundred plus miles to go.

With these new rules in place, I asked Wilma and Jim if I could limit my trips to Fort Jackson. A new driver, Lee, took over the route. Not only was he a lot younger than I, but as a former Marine, he loved making the trip to his old stomping grounds at Parris Island. After that, instead of driving every Monday to Parris Island, I just occasionally filled in for Lee.

The Rockslide

The eleven o'clock television news showed a huge rockslide on I-40 near the Tennessee/North Carolina line. I watched the video and realized the boulders covering all four lanes of the interstate had been hanging above as I drove back and forth beneath them—several hundred times. The detour around the rockslide took I-81 north to Johnson City, Tennessee, then south on I-26 to Asheville, North Carolina. With snow in the mountains, there was beauty but also driving danger. *My God was with me every mile of the way.*

The newsman on television said, "The cleanup will take at least three months." It was six months, while I detoured more than an hour in each direction, before the highway finally reopened. I welcomed the extra couple hours to rest after each trip.

Most of the time, I felt sad when my troops reached their destinations. With a good group of young men and women, the jokes would fly and relationships built. I just wanted to hold onto them and not let them go, to see how they grew and changed. Then there were times—very few—when I couldn't wait to see them get out of the van. Either way, each new week brought new people and new adventures. There was no job in the world like it.

CHAPTER 9

JAMES THE SILENT

Up until that point, all the trips talked about have been great, and they were all been about how respectful my troops were. But I finally ran into one that was the worst one of all—and here's the reason why.

I picked up James at MEPS and we headed out to Fort Knox. It was clear right off that he was different. When I asked him a question, he would answer with a short yes or no, then just stare out the window.

A slow hour passed as I tried to draw him into my world. Then I quit asking questions and he fell asleep. Three hours later, I had to wake him up as we approached Cracker Barrel for our meal. Inside, we sat down to eat. James immediately picked up the wooden triangle puzzle that was on the table and began to play with it. He gave the waitress his order without looking at her. When our food arrived, we ate and sat for an hour in total silence. This was a first for me, and it drove me nuts.

As we got back into the van and on the road, I couldn't stand it any longer. I said a silent prayer that God would allow me to keep my cool and not say the wrong thing. Then I just let go.

"Young man," I said. "You're not going to like what I have to say next. But if you don't start to open up, at least to your fellow soldiers, and try to get along with them, you will not make it in this man's Army!" I was correct. He didn't like what I said—but it didn't seem to affect him in any way. There was no indication he heard me at all. He didn't say a word, just continued to stare out the window. Not another word was spoken between us until we pulled up at the reception center at Fort Knox.

When it was time to let James out of the van I tried one more time to reach out to him. He had shown no respect for me, but I was still concerned about him. "James," I said. "May I say a prayer for you?" He looked at me with a pitying but resolute expression and said, "Do what you have to do."

I really felt sorry for him. I was at a loss for words. I didn't know how to help him, but I did say that prayer. Although I normally feel the Holy Spirit present during my prayers, this time was an exception. At the end of the short prayer, James got out of the van and was gone. I often wonder where he is today? *God bless you, James.*

I hoped I had done everything I could have for James. I'm sure I haven't always met my goals, God knows I've always tried. The job was not really a *job* but an opportunity to serve God in the way He chose to lead me.

CHAPTER 10

A ROSE BY ANY OTHER NAME

On another trip I drove two people to Fort Knox. Their names were Timmy and Cory. Cory crawled into the back of the van and went to sleep. Timmy rode up front with me. He wanted to talk rather than sleep. We had a good trip, exchanging stories about our families. He had been divorced for some time, and he started telling me about a great girl he met at his National Guard unit. It was obvious he liked her a lot and talked about her just about the whole trip, but I wasn't bored. As he described her, she had a bubbly personality. He talked about how pretty she was, as a young man in love has a tendency to do. He said her name was K.C. However, because of what happened later, I gave her a new name—Rose, so I'll call her Rose here.

Timmy had two themes in his conversation—his stories about Rose and how he wanted to get closer to God. He told me he'd be going to chapel every Sunday. Then he'd talk about Rose's upcoming birthday. He had a birthday card for her but didn't have a stamp, so he asked me if I would mail it for him when I got home. I promised I would and, as I always did, asked him to write to me if there was anything else I could do for him. A month later I received a letter from Timmy. In his letter he wrote the following words:

Dear Terry,

I hope that you remember me. My name is Timmy L——. We had a conversation about God on the way to Fort Knox. I read *Psalms 91* all the time, and it gives me a lot of hope for all that I'm going through. I want to thank you for all your prayers, and for praying for me before you dropped me off. It's no mistake that God puts people like you in my way to view a blessing here on earth, and for that I am thankful. Sometimes, we are the only "Jesus" some people will ever see here on earth. I told you a little bit about my girlfriend, K.C. [*No Timmy, you told me a lot about your girlfriend!*]

His letter went on to tell me that K.C. would be shipping out to Fort Jackson in a month. He asked if it would be possible for me to arrange to be the driver on the day she went down. I wrote back, and told him he should tell her I'd do all I could to be working on that day.

Timmy enclosed a five-dollar bill in his next letter and asked me to buy a rose to give to his girl. He also gave me a ship date of May 19. I kept that letter with me for over three weeks, waiting for the date to arrive. I also made special arrangements so I would be working on the day.

May 19th came and I left early so I'd have time to stop at the florist shop. I went in, placed the five-dollar bill on the counter and told the clerk the story. She picked out a perfect rose and wrapped it in some kind of pretty green paper.

When I arrived at MEPS, I asked if Rose was shipping to Fort Jackson that day. "No, she ships tomorrow!" *Great! All my plans derailed.* So, I called Wilma who scheduled our runs and asked if I could drive to Fort Jackson the next day. She said they'd already planned a trip to Fort Knox the next day for me, because Lee, the new man, had never driven to Fort Knox. So, I asked Jim, my boss, to put the rose in the cooler to wait. Someone else would get to present Rose with her rose.

Still thinking about my promise to Timmy, when I arrived at MEPS the next day. I asked Skip at the information desk where I could find K.C. He said she was in the game room. I retrieved the rose from the cooler and walked in with it in my hand. There were only four people in the room. Only one, sitting in the corner alone, could have been the beautiful girl Timmy described.

Seeing a stranger approaching with a rose in his hand, she looked from the rose to me. I expected to see joy, I suppose, but the more I explained, the more her confusion seemed to grow. Then it was her turn to explain. She assured me Timmy was nothing more than a good friend. She said she knew who he was, but she had a boyfriend. Nevertheless, she accepted the rose and thanked me for everything I had done to bring it to her. I gave her one of my cards. She said she'd write to me later on, but she never did. It was as though I'd been in the middle of a love plot, and I felt somewhat betrayed by young Timmy who put me into such an embarrassing position.

Later in the week I called Lee and asked him about the trip to Fort Jackson with Rose aboard. He said she cried a lot during the trip, and that she held on to the rose the whole way.

CHAPTER 11

ALAN THE BUDDHIST

The day dawned a beautiful Tennessee Monday morning with plenty of sunshine. With ten hours sleep under my belt, I was feeling great! However, a couple of changes were in store for me. First of all, I had been scheduled to drive to Fort Jackson, but the company changed my direction from south to north. That was okay; I knew if God wanted me to go to Fort Knox, He must have someone special for me to meet there.

Ordinarily, on a run to Fort Jackson I'd have been driving the van we called *The Big Green Ugly*. However, when all the vehicles were in use the company rented me a 2009 Chevy Tahoe SUV. It was a fine vehicle, and all I could think was that God was being really good to me.

The Tahoe had buttons and switches everywhere. When I stopped for gas I couldn't find the button to open the outside fuel compartment. Since there was a button for everything else, I expected to find one for this. After spending five minutes looking for the button, with no luck, I gave up and went back around just to puzzle over it one more time. I pushed on the gas tank door and it opened. Go figure!

This trip to Fort Knox was one of the most interesting. Alan and three other recruits were waiting at MEPS for a ride to the airport for the new guys to catch an early flight. After that it was just the two of us. We headed up I-40 then onto I-75 north. Most of my Army guys were very laid back. All they could think about was getting some sleep or wondering when they'd get their next smoke. The question they asked most often was, "Sir, when is our next stop?"

Alan was different. He made a ten minute telephone call to his wife then put out his hand for me to shake and said, "Hello, my name is Alan. What's your name?" I knew right then I was in for a good trip. I told him he could get in the back and take a nap if he wanted to, but he said he'd rather sit up front and talk to me.

After some small talk about family and friends, he told me his father was a Pentecostal minister and his wife's grandfather was a Baptist preacher. I said, "Well, I guess that makes you a born-again Christian?" His answer? "No, I'm a Buddhist!"

You could have knocked me over with a feather. *So much for having a good Christian conversation. God, is this a test?* As we made our way to I-75 north, we began to talk about our different religions. I asked him how he would go about converting me if I was interested in becoming a Buddhist. He said he wouldn't do such a thing, because they didn't believe in trying to convert people to their beliefs. He said he loved talking about different religions and would love to discuss any and all questions about being a Buddhist—in a non-threatening way.

I found Alan easy to talk to and it was fun. For the next hour we bounced questions back and forth off each other, and no questions were off limits. *Am I passing your test, Lord?*

I took a cell phone call from Connie, and when I looked at Alan he was fast asleep. I guessed his brain needed a rest from our question and answer session. He slept for about forty minutes until his cell phone woke him. When he finished the call he said, "Let's see, we were talking about heaven and hell when your phone rang?" *Wow, he really does like talking about this stuff!*

So, we picked up where we'd left off earlier. He said he didn't believe in heaven and hell, that when you died you just lay around forever. Whether that's what all Buddhists believe, I don't know, but for the next half hour I talked to him about the wonderful prospect believers faced when we died. Since his dad was a preacher, I guess he'd heard it all before. He did agree, however, that he was enjoying our talk—and I surely was.

If I could remember every detail of our conversation, I could fill up several pages but I do remember one thing in particular. I said to Alan, "You can believe this if you want to, but last night before I went to sleep I said a prayer for you. The plan was for me to drive to Fort Jackson. When I called to confirm the schedule, for some reason they had changed my trip. Thinking I would be going to Fort Jackson, I had prayed for God to bless whomever I would be driving to basic training, that they'd be open to hearing the message He'd want to give to them. Then I asked Alan, "Do you believe it was by accident our paths crossed today?" After a short pause he said, "I guess it is possible there is a divine intervention!" *Wow! Does that sound like a Buddhist talking?* It's not what I would expect to hear.

Soon it was time to make our usual stop at Cracker Barrel. We kept talking all through the meal. Back on the road, we had forty-five minutes or so before arriving at Fort Knox. During that time, Alan showed me pictures of his family, including one of a beautiful three-year-old girl who looked just like her mother. My next words must have come straight from God. They left my heart without being formed in my brain. I said, "I believe that either your little three-year-old or your unborn child will sometime in your life bring you back to Christ!"

There was a short pause. I thought I saw tears in his eyes as he said, "You know, you could be right!" I had to hold back my own tears. *Thank you, God, for this great day. I think I've passed your test.*

For the rest of the trip not a word was spoken. There was peace in the van. We arrived at the reception center. I put the van in park, looked over at Alan and asked if I could say a prayer for him. He gave me a big smile and said, "Please do!"

I prayed for Alan, as I do all my troops, from the heart. Afterwards, I asked if he would write to let me know how things were going at basic training. He said he would. I told him about the book I was writing, and he said, "Do you think you might find a paragraph in your book for me?" I told him, "No, you are going to get a whole chapter!" We both had a good laugh over that.

His last words to me were, "Terry, I am so glad we met, and I hope someday we'll meet again!" At the time I began to write this chapter, it had been over six months, and I had not received a letter from him.

Dear God, he is in your hands now. Please bless Alan and keep him safe. Amen.

CHAPTER 12

UP IN SMOKE

The title of this chapter came mostly from the way my troops smoked cigarettes or dipped snuff. I could spot the smokers right away. They'd approach me with a smile and say "Sir, when is our next stop?" My reply was, "You're a smoker, aren't you?" With a shocked look they'd ask how I knew. Then they'd want to know, "Can we smoke on the van?"

"No smoking or dipping in the van! We'll stop shortly for gas and you can smoke then," I'd say, with what I hoped sounded like authority. And like a kid on Christmas morning they'd answer, "Thank you, sir. We love you!" They would have been without a cigarette or dip since six that morning, and the desire for nicotine had grown strong. They knew their smoking days were coming to an end soon, so they cherished every opportunity they could get. Some feared they were going to be stuck in the van all day without a break. The addiction to tobacco could be a serious problem for a future soldier. I've transported well over a thousand troops in a three-year period of time. Not one person ever tried to sneak a cigarette or take a dip while we were en route.

One day I checked my rear view mirror just to keep an eye on the happenings in the back and saw a young man spitting something into a Mountain Dew bottle. He did this several times. I thought *surely, he is not violating my "no dipping rule!"* But I kept my cool. When we stopped for our usual halfway point break outside of Asheville, North Carolina, I waited until everyone left *The Big Green Ugly*. Then I climbed into the back of the van, on a mission to find that Mountain Dew bottle. It didn't take long to find it under a bench seat. I took a deep breath and opened the bottle to find—the remains of chewed up sunflower seeds.

I have never smoked. Well, okay, I have smoked a few "It's a Girl" and "It's a Boy" cigars. My father was a heavy smoker. He smoked over a pack of cigarettes a day. Even as a teenager I couldn't understand why anyone would waste twenty-five cents on a pack of cigarettes when they could have bought an RC Cola and a Moon Pie!

I heard stories all the time from the recruits, both men and women, of how they had smoked since a very young age. They'd also tell me that, for them, it was a precursor to getting into drugs and alcohol.

Just knowing that in a few short hours they would be taking their last puff, something prompted them to smoke as many as they could in the short amount of time they had left. Once, when we were at our last stop before reaching Fort Jackson, one recruit had five cigarettes left and only a few minutes to smoke them before we departed. He placed all five cigarettes in a circle and put them all in his mouth at the same time and lit them up. You talk about a nicotine high!

I've received a few letters thanking me for allowing them the freedom to smoke on the trip. I tried to understand the power of such an addiction in their young lives. Although I didn't smoke while I was in the Army, I'd have been able to because back then it was permissible. As you watch some of the older movies you can see that they allowed the troops to "light up" or "smoke 'em if you got 'em!" Having more than two smokers on a trip could add as much a half an hour to the total time to the total trip time.

One recruit was bragging to the rest of the group how his wife didn't mind if he dipped. I asked him "What happens when you go to kiss her?" "No problem," he replied. "She just takes her dip out and then we kiss!"

I've watched smokers either eat their meal really fast, or in some cases not at all, just so they could devote all the mealtime to a last smoke. As they would take the last puff, I'd ask them "Are you going to quit for good now?" Most of them said they were planning to do just that. Others told me they'd be lighting up on their way home from basic training. I have received letters confirming both statements.

I think this "devil stick" could have such a hold on them for so long they were glad a force bigger than they would be forcing them to quit. I knew it wouldn't be easy; however, "the man in the green round hat" would be keeping them so busy maybe the last thing on their minds would be a cigarette.

I would not buy my troops cigarettes or dip. Sometimes, when we were at Shoney's and someone didn't have a cigarette, it was okay to accept one from the waitress. Also if they had any leftover cigarettes, I would allow them to leave the cigarettes with their waitress instead of throwing them in the trash.

On trips to Fort Knox, my last stop would be at the Marathon filling station right outside the base. If any of the troops needed a last nicotine stick there, Vicky would always gladly give them one. In turn, they sometimes left behind unsmoked cigarettes. She was always happy to see the troops and never failed to greet them with a smile.

This was also a favorite stop of my boss, Jim Cline when he made his many trips to Fort Knox. Vicky would always ask, "How is Pops doing?" When Jim became sick, Vicky asked for Pops' telephone number so she could call and cheer him. Then came the day that I had to tell her Pops had passed away. She wept. After she regained her composure, she told me that many years ago, Jim gave her a pretty rose. "Terry," she said. "I still have the rose pressed in a book." I could see in her eyes how their friendship had grown over the years.

CHAPTER 13

FUNNY HAPPENINGS
ON THE WAY TO BASIC TRAINING

Each of my trips to basic training was special in its own way. Even if nothing funny or out of the ordinary happened, I still enjoyed the trip. Of course there were often events and happenings that stood out, and it's always fun to recount them. All of them are true to the best of my recollection and the only things I've changed are a few names.

Once with a vanload of Marines, I made the last rest stop of the trip at the Texaco station twenty-five miles from Parris Island. As usual, just before getting back on the road I handed out my business cards, the ones with the symbol of the cross and the words *Psalm91* in the upper left corner. A few minutes later, with everyone cutting up and having fun, someone let out a cuss word. Cory, who was sitting way in back, hollered in his molasses-slow Southern drawl, "Shut up, man! The man just gave you a church card!"

The offending person excused himself with, "I said that word before he gave me the church card."

The power of the cross!

Tunnel Vision

Going down I-40 (before the big rock slide of January 31, 2012), the highway passes through two tunnels. Mary Ann had fallen asleep while riding in the front passenger seat. She had been out of it for a while as we entered the first tunnel. About half way through she woke up, and began to hyperventilate. When we emerged from the second tunnel, she said,

"I woke up and saw the dark tunnel and those small interior lights and thought I had died. I didn't know if I was going to heaven or hell!"

When we were five minutes from the gate of Fort Jackson, her cell phone rang. She listened for about thirty seconds and then cried out, sobbing. After she hung up I asked if she was okay. "My grandmother just died," she said.

We arrived at the reception center at Fort Jackson, all the recruits got out of the van except Mary Ann. I pulled the drill sergeant aside and explained what had happened. While he called his first sergeant, I went back to see how Mary Ann was doing. She had calmed down and began to give me a little more information. As it turned out, it was not *her* grandmother who died but her husband's grandmother. "I was very close to her," she said. Then she said she no longer lived with her husband and added, "I don't like him anymore."

When I gave the drill sergeant the corrected information, he barked, "Young lady, get out of this van. You're not going anywhere!" Mary Ann's first day in the Army was not getting off to a very good start, but my job was done.

Hey, Dude

On a trip to Fort Knox a young man named Ron called everybody Dude. During the five-hour trip he must have used the word at least thirty times. He called me Dude, the one other person with us was Dude, and even people we passed on the Interstate were Dude. Finally, I asked him, "Why do you call everybody Dude?" He answered "Oh, Dude, I spent a few years in California and we called everybody Dude!"

In due time, I dropped Ron and the others off at Fort Knox. A few days later, I had two more recruits to take to Fort Knox and I had to walk them to a different location, through a large courtyard where at least two hundred soldiers stood at attention. They all looked too scared to move. Dressed in summer black shorts, brand new tennis shoes, and gray tee shirts with the word Army across their chests, they looked like clones.

As we walked in front of them we heard a series of wolf whistles, which the drill sergeant quickly put a stop to. The two recruits and I went into one of the old buildings where I left them with their drill sergeant. Leaving the building to return to the van, I had to walk past the formation again. As I cleared the last row a voice called out softly, "Hey, Dude!"

Blue Grass

The innocence of some of the young recruits was always surprising and entertaining. Young Jimmy rode up front with me on one trip to Fort Knox. Looking out the window he said, "My mama told me that the grass was blue here in Kentucky! It ain't blue. *It's green.*" He made a call on his cell phone. "Mama," he said, "You told me the grass was blue up here in Kentucky. It ain't blue, it's green, just like it is at our house!" I thought about all the discoveries Jimmy was about to make—all of them more momentous than finding out Kentucky grass wasn't blue.

The Mexican Rap Channel

Sometimes funny things happened even when no recruits were in the van. On the way home from Fort Knox, with everything going fine, I was in the last two hours of the trip. Mark Levin's talk show was on the radio, and he was doing his usual lambasting of a caller about something or other. Fifty miles from the Jellico Mountain on the Tennessee/Kentucky border, the radio suddenly went off all by itself. When it came back on I pushed the seek button and it stopped on a religious station. I tried to get back to the Levin show, but a religious station kept coming up, the same one on all the preset buttons. This was like a scene out of *Close Encounters Of The Third Kind!* No matter what I did I could not get it to change the station. The radio went off and on several times by itself.

I called Wilma to tell her the radio was broken. She started writing down everything just as I told it to her. Being somewhat of a practical joker, I thought I'd have a little fun with her. When I got to the part about the channel being stuck, I changed my story just a little bit. "And it's stuck on the Mexican rap channel! In three years, I had never heard Wilma laugh as hard as she laughed about that. I didn't tell her any different, either. From then on, all I'd have to do was mention the Mexican rap channel to make her laugh. As every successful practical joke does, this one grew and spread among the crew. The next day at MEPS, Skip asked if I'd heard any good Mexican rap songs lately.

By the way, when I stopped at the rest area and returned to the van, the radio reset itself—so I got to listen to the rest of the Mark Levin Show—and he wasn't talking about ghosts or UFOs.

Miniskirt and Pantyhose

All the funny things aren't necessarily coming from inside the van, though. When I pulled into the Pilot gas station to stretch my legs, top off the gas tank and get a cup of their good coffee, the troops and I got a show we never in the world expected to see.

Some of the recruits on this trip were women, and as I stopped at pump number six, one of them let out a surprised hoot, "Oh my gosh! Look at that man! He has on a mini skirt—and he's wearing pantyhose." After I'd convinced them to tone it down, we all got out of the van. Lo and behold, there stood a man in his thirties, dressed in a blue t-shirt, a navy blue miniskirt that covered about half his manly-looking, pantyhose-covered legs, and with all this, he wore a pair of tennis shoes. We watched as he finished pumping gas, got into his car and drove away. He must have been used to the stares, but my troops could hardly contain their laughter.

It's Not What You Think

It was rare to need two vans to transport the recruits on one day. But one time on a trip to Parris Island, I drove *The Big Gray Ugly* with a full load of fourteen recruits, followed by Steve with four more in the minivan.

At the last stop, at the Texaco station, everyone waited their turn to visit the small restrooms. Most of us stood outside laughing, talking, and, of course, the smokers were smoking. A handful of them went in to purchase bottles of water and snacks. Suddenly one of the guys let out a wolf whistle that snowballed into a scene that would make a construction worker proud. "Okay, guys," I cautioned. "Be cool. Remember who you are and where you're going!"

What caused the uproar was a woman sporting long black hair and wearing tight jeans. She got out of an older model Lincoln with a man in the driver's seat and headed inside the gas station. Not a bit bothered by the crude attention, she responded to the wolf calls with a big smile and a, "Hey, Baby!"

Just when I'd got my pack of wolves back to normal, the door opened and she came out. The wolves started howling again. Holding a twelve pack of beer in one hand and responding to the wolf calls with a wave, she flashed another big smile and called out, "Bye, baby!"

As the Lincoln Town Car drove out of sight, I looked inside the gas station and noticed several of our guys inside talking to Dustin the clerk. He said something that caused them to laugh. When they came out I asked, "What was so funny?" Only one person could stop laughing enough to stutter out the words, "That girl was a guy!"

While everybody dealt with the fact that they had been lusting after a man, I went inside and talked to Dustin. He told me this was the second time that night the guy had been in the store. Each time he had asked for ID for the beer—and the woman's ID had shown a picture of a man with an open shirt and a hairy chest!

Sir, I Have To Go To The Bathroom Again

We all piled back into the vans and headed on to Parris Island, just thirty miles away. Everyone was still talking about the encounter at the gas station, and the jokes were flying. With only a couple more miles to go, I heard James call out from the back of the van, "Sir, I have to go to the bathroom again!" No one else said a word. We had passed all of the restroom stops. Since there was only one person with the problem I decided to look for a safe out-of-the-way place so this one young man would be able to get on base with an empty bladder.

The last chance to pull off happened to be the parking lot of a Baptist church sitting a hundred yards off the main road. We pulled up to the dimly lit parking lot. I checked the rear view mirror to see that Steve had his right blinker on and was following us. I parked as far as possible from the security light at the end of the lot. There didn't seem to be any surveillance cameras on the roof of the church, and I was glad it was Monday night—not Wednesday service night. James made his way out of the van and headed for the far end of the darkened parking lot.

Then, just like a bunch of kids, when one needed to go, they all needed to go! I heard, "Oh man, I gotta go to!" and, "Me too!" One by one for the next several seconds, thirteen people piled out the side door and took their places side-by-side next to James. When I looked at Steve's minivan, four more emerged and then there were seventeen lined up. Fortunately, we didn't have any women on that trip. Steve and I just stood there laughing at the row of men so similar to the little garden fountain figures with water cascading out front.

Sir, You Scared Me To Death

One day, Divus was the last person to get on the van at MEPS. Divus was a small man with a nice smile and pearly white teeth showing up well against his dark skin. He recognized me and said, in a soft Southern Tennessee drawl, "Sir, you took me to basic training last year and you scared me to death!" I was shocked at this and wasn't sure I wanted to hear the rest, but I asked anyhow, "How did I scare you? Was it my driving?"

He was still smiling when he said, "No, sir, it wasn't your driving at all! When we got to Fort Jackson last year, you said a prayer for me in the name of the Lord Jesus and it scared me to death. I thought it must really be bad here at Fort Jackson for you to say a prayer in the name of the Lord Jesus."

We had a really good trip that day and after passing through the gate at Fort Jackson, I pulled over at my favorite prayer spot. I don't know what purpose the Army had for this little bit of real estate, but I had turned it into a prayer stop. The sun had just gone down. The last of the day's light was trying to creep into the van. I turned around to begin and my gaze fixed on Divus. He was leaning over with his hands on the back of the bench seat in front of him. With his hands folded in the prayer position, he was watching me. His voice carried all the way from the back of the van as he gave me that beautiful, pearly smile and said, with obvious humor in his voice, "I'm ready for you this time, sir!"

CHAPTER 14

THE BIG GRAY UGLY RETIRES

The Big Gray Ugly was a 2002 Dodge fifteen-passenger van, and it was finally time for it to retire. Up until then, I had made several trips to Parris Island, Fort Jackson, and Fort Knox without any problems or breakdowns. The company had just put in a "brand new" rebuilt transmission just a week before, and I was expecting no trouble.

After dropping off a few people at the McGhee-Tyson Airport in Knoxville, I headed to Parris Island with several Marine recruits. A couple of miles down the road, the transmission started slipping and the van stopped moving forward. It was like being in neutral. My first thought was, "Surely it couldn't be that "brand new" rebuilt transmission they just put in a week ago."

I pulled to the side of the road and called the office. Tony, one of the owners, answered the phone. He wasn't happy but said he'd be there in ten minutes. He said we'd have to wait until they could locate a van to rent. An hour passed before Tony pulled up in a brand new, white Ford fifteen-passenger van. My reaction was, *"Wow! I'm gonna like this!"*

Everything went great on the way down. Because of the breakdown I was running a couple of hours late. On the way back, I made the rest stop just north of Columbia. Then, fifteen minutes later, I felt an urge to relieve myself again. "Rats!" I thought. It was 2:30 in the morning and no one around, so I just pulled over to the side of the road, like men sometimes do, and found a safe place at the side of the road.

It was early March with warm days and cool nights. The weather forecast said it was going down to the low forties with a cool breeze. So, thinking to keep the van warm I left the engine running. When I returned, I found the door locked. In that instant of disbelief my short-term memory kicked in, and I remembered hearing a click when I shut the door. I ran around the van desperately trying the doors and praying. *No such luck! Now what was I going to do?*

My jacket would have felt pretty good right about then, but it was in the van—with my cell phone. Under any other circumstances, this would have been a pleasant spring night to be out, bright stars in a clear sky and all, but I was in a pickle. I was locked out of the van, starting to feel the effects of the chilly weather, alone on a four-lane interstate in the wee hours of the morning.

I saw a semi truck coming down the hill, and I thought surely it would stop; so I stood in the slow lane waving my arms. His blinker went on, but it was the left one, and I watched him drive on past. I kept trying to flag someone down, but no one would stop.

Finally, since my way wasn't working, I decided to ask for God's help. When I opened my eyes, there was a car stopped fifty feet away. I ran up and looked through the closed window at the woman inside. She mouthed the words, "Do you need help?"

I told her I'd locked the keys in the van with the engine running and asked her to call the highway patrol. I was shivering in the early morning air, and it was music to my ears when the window went down and she said, "Would you like to get in the car and warm up?"

Once inside, I said, "May I ask why you stopped on a lonely road at three in the morning for a man you didn't know?" Her answer explained the nurse's uniform she wore. "I just finished my shift at the emergency room, and you looked like you needed help." She smiled and added, "I believe in guardian angels that protect me." I told her, "I believe in guardian angels, too—and you've been mine."

After ten minutes or so of small talk, we saw not one, but two, South Carolina Highway Patrol cars pull up, blue lights flashing. I got out of her car, and she drove away.

I got in the patrol car and told the officer I needed a locksmith. He radioed for one. I sat in the back seat of the patrol trying to make small talk with the officer, but he wanted no part of it. He answered my questions with a clipped yes or no. A half hour passed, with only the radio transmission chatter telling of stopped cars or other patrolmen going on break. Finally the locksmith showed up, and I transferred from the patrol car to the tow truck. Within five minutes I was back on the road in the nice warm van. After all, the heater had been running for an hour and a half.

The time I thought to save by stopping on the side of the road had cost me over an hour. I checked the gas gauge. It was time to get off at the next exit to get gas. I decided maybe I'd better visit the restroom while I was there.

My next workday, I was hoping to hear the news *The Big Gray Ugly* would be retiring and the replacement for the transmission wasn't a match. Instead, I was told all it needed was a few adjustments of some gears and then it would be good as new.

Six months later *The Big Gray Ugly* broke down again. The alternator went out in Clinton, coming back from Fort Jackson, South Carolina. It happened two hundred miles from home this time, and I had to spend the night in a motel. The next day I arranged to have the van towed to a garage for repairs, and before long I was on my way home again.

Soon after, I was scheduled to drive *The Big Gray* Ugly once again. Before even leaving MEPS, the ignition made an odd noise when I turned the key. With my limited knowledge of mechanics I didn't know it was the starter going out. I dutifully reported it to headquarters and was told everything would be all right, that it could be repaired when I got back.

I had four young men going to Fort Jackson and two for Parris Island. After each stop, when I turned the key to start up again, the noise returned. It was 7:00 p.m. when we pulled up at the front gate at Fort Jackson, right on time, but that's where the van stopped—deader than a doornail. The guard and troops pushed it off to the side.

I called Wilma and gave her the good news—*The Big Gray Ugly* was stranded at the front gate of Fort Jackson. She wasn't happy, but neither was I. Her orders were—I was to have the gate guard call for someone to pick up the four recruits to deliver to the reception center. Then I was to call a cab for the rest of us to go to the airport. From there we would continue in a rental car.

Trying to find an airport car rental at midnight had the potential for disaster. Nevertheless, the clerk finally found one newly returned that hadn't yet been processed. We didn't care. Two and a half hours later, I turned my troops over to their new friend in the Smokey the Bear hat and headed home.

It was almost 3:00 a.m., more than five hours later than I would normally leave Parris Island. *What a night!* Now I still had an eight-hour trip home. That would give me plenty of time to think about what I was going to tell my boss. *I'd had it with The Big Gray Ugly.*

I-26 was a lonely road at 4:00 in the morning. I had to laugh out loud as I passed the place where I locked my keys in the van with the engine running. About then I noticed the gas gauge was almost on empty. I needed some coffee, *and I had to go to the restroom*!

Back on the road with a full tank of gas, a hot cup of coffee and an empty bladder I started to get my thoughts together. This was the last trip I would take in that van. The words kept running through my head: *Either The Big Gray Ugly goes—or I go!*

I couldn't help thinking, too, how much I loved this job. I could almost hear my voice saying it. Then the voices came back: *However, there comes a time when one has to take a stand!*

I had to take one more power nap, so it was 11:00 a.m. when I finally made it home—a twenty-two hour workday. Connie said, "I just wish you didn't like this job as well as you do. I worry about you so much." She was right. She did worry, and sometimes I did love this job too much.

Children often say when asked why they did something, "I just couldn't help it!" I remember saying it myself when I was young. In a way that's how I felt about the driving job. I was moved by my God to drive as many trips as possible, and I just couldn't help myself. There was no way to tell which recruit would be helped by God's message. A simple prayer or a few words on a card, anything might change a life.

After a good rest in my own bed I was ready to confront the company about retiring *The Big Gray Ugly*. I called Wilma to talk about the events of the day. She started right off to tell me how great I had handled everything and how I'd done everything right. She said she was sorry for all the trouble I'd gone through. It didn't hurt a bit when she added there'd be an extra twenty-five dollars on my next check! Maybe it was understandable that I thought I'd just maybe better wait until after payday to state my case.

Thinking back over the day, though, I decided it couldn't wait. I told Wilma she might not be so happy with me when she heard what else I had to say. For the next few minutes I laid it out for her in no uncertain terms. She had a feeble comeback, something about how the company had kept up the maintenance even though the van had 550,000 miles on it. However, I think the message finally sank in when I said, unequivocally, "I refuse to drive that piece of junk again! Either it goes or I go!"

The bottom line was they agreed to park *The Big Gray Ugly* and, to this day, that old gray van, its gray paint faded almost to white, is resting in peace in Tony's front yard. *Hey, after all, this is Tennessee!*

CHAPTER 15

SHONEY'S

Let's Eat

"Sir, where are we going to stop and eat?" I loved it when I heard that question. I got to have some fun with my troops. I'd say, "What day is today?" "Today is Monday. Sir." I'd try to keep a straight face. "Well, on Mondays and Wednesdays, we eat at Shoney's, and on Tuesdays and Thursdays we eat at Hooters!" Disappointed, their voices would plead, "Can't we eat at Hooters today?"

"What day is today?" I'd say again. "Monday, sir." The disappointment in their voices was apparent. *They don't get it, yet. Is this a blonde joke?* So, I'd repeat, "On Mondays and Wednesdays we eat at Shoney's, and on Tuesdays and Thursdays we eat at Hooters! Now, what day is today?" By this time some of the troops would catch on and they'd flash me a big smile. Not everyone was happy about it, though. One of the Marine recruits didn't like looking foolish. He said, "That's not funny!"

Most of the guys, enjoying the joke and happy to join in, wouldn't let it drop, though, and kept calling out things like, "I love Hooters' food!" or "I hate Hooters' food!" One even hollered, "I like to get Hooters' food for take out!" This got a huge roar of laughter.

On the way to Fort Jackson or Parris Island we almost always pulled off at exit 113, just outside Columbia, South Carolina, to eat at Shoney's. After being cooped up in a van with me for four or five hours, they were ready to stretch out and have a good meal. Tuesdays were steak-on-the-grill night. Chris, one of the managers, would be standing at the big propane grill cooking up some of the best T-bone and rib eye steaks in the South. When I'd pull into the parking lot and hit the down button on the window,

I didn't have to say a word. Chris would look up and say, "Hey, rib eye medium well, gotcha!"

I'd been going to this Shoney's for over two years, and even a lot of the regular customers recognized me. The wait staff usually greeted me with a chorus of "Hey baby, how you doing?" or "Hi, Mr. Terry, good to see you!" or "Do you have a large group tonight?" It was a lot like walking onto the set of the television show, *Cheers* because everybody knew my name.

Shoney's was the place where my troops could unwind. Even the quiet ones would open up and start talking once we were seated. We were generally there about an hour. The Army people weren't always happy to learn they were only fifteen minutes from Fort Jackson. However the Marines were happy to have another three hours of freedom to look forward to before reaching Parris Island.

A Nickel Question And A Dollar Answer

If anything out of the ordinary happens, it would usually be at Shoney's. On one trip, I had two women and one man, going to Fort Jackson. Paul had spent four years in the Marines. Six months before he'd been kicked out for, among other things, sleeping on guard duty. The Marines wouldn't take him back so he joined the Army. The two women, Betty and Melissa, knew he had served time in the military, and they asked question after question about basic training. He gave them detailed answers.

We arrived at Shoney's and everything was going fine. When the food came, Betty politely bowed her head and said a quiet grace. After she finished Melissa asked Paul another nickel question and Paul gave her a dollar answer. The next thing I knew, quiet, demure Betty came up out of her seat and leaned across the table at Paul. She took her middle finger and placed it across his mouth and told him to *shut the * * * up!* Then she said, "I have listened to your mouth for five hours and I am sick of it!"

Paul was sitting next to me. He looked at me and said, "I don't think she likes me!" Betty looked him straight in the eye and said, "No, I don't!" After a few seconds, I broke the tension, "Would someone please pass the salt?"

A year later to the day, I had another group going to Fort Jackson. This time one of the women said, "Do you remember taking me down to basic training this time last year?"

I told her she'd have to refresh my memory and asked, "Did anything out of the ordinary happen?" She laughed out loud and recounted the story about the ex-Marine and a girl named Betty. "I'm Melissa! I was the quiet one!"

Melissa figured in another one of my memories about Shoney's. She was one of those people who had to have everything in its proper order or it would drive her crazy. As we drove along, I listened to many stories about her life and how she must have everything perfect. When we neared Shoney's, I thought she'd be good at the task of collecting all of the checks from the rest of the troops and keeping track of them. She readily accepted the job.

After our meal she handed me the checks and said, "Here you are. I put them in alphabetic order for you!" Being the mischievous person I am, I thanked her, picked up the checks and began to shuffle them like a deck of cards. Melissa panicked. "Sir, please don't do that. Now I'll have to do it all over again!" Well, *I* thought it was funny.

I'm Sorry If I Got You In Trouble!

Most of my stories had a good ending. Here is one that did not. This was one of my first trips to Parris Island. We stopped at Shoney's for our meal. One of the waiters at Shoney's (who is no longer working there) had an earring in each ear. After the meal was complete and everyone was sitting around talking, two of the Marines asked if they could go next door to buy some cigarettes. Ten minutes later, the manager took me to the side and said we had a problem. She said that the two young men who left made a comment about the waiter who was wearing the earring. They asked one of the waitresses if he was gay and she told them he was. The young man said, "Well, he doesn't belong here!" The waiter heard the conversation and was upset by it. I told the manager I would make him apologize.

She told me she had already smoothed everything over. She said, "The only thing I ask is that you tell the drill instructor when you get to Parris Island!" I met the two young men coming across the parking lot and asked which one made the comment to the waitress. Immediately, one of them spoke up, "I did, sir. I take full responsibility for it!" He offered to go and apologize, but I told him to just get in the van.

Five miles from Parris Island, the young man who had caused the problem spoke up. "Terry, man, I'm sorry if I got you in trouble!" I told him, "I'm not in trouble but I have to tell your drill instructor when we get to Parris Island!" We pulled up to the Welcome Center and I went inside to retrieve the drill instructor. I told him the story. He said he'd take care of it. I found out later that the recruit spent his first seventeen days in the brig.

My Friend Scottie

On a trip when I was taking just one person to Fort Jackson we were seated across from a fairly large man in a wheelchair. He was cutting up with the waitresses, smiling continuously. At one point our eyes met. I smiled at him and got an even bigger smile in return. He introduced himself as Scottie. He said he didn't know my name but he knew that I transported the troops to basic training. I introduced myself, and it was the start of an ongoing friendship. Scottie told me he was a ten-year veteran of the Army. He had served as an Army Ranger. After leaving the Army, he went to work for a law enforcement agency. In the line of duty, he was shot and nearly died. While he was in the hospital he developed a rare blood disease, and that was the reason he was in the wheelchair—and would be for the rest of his life.

Scottie was one of the most remarkable men I'd ever met. He owned his own company, and traveled by himself in a special van revamped for his wheelchair. Every time he had business in Columbia he always ate at Shoney's and lodged at the motel next door.

Scottie always took time to talk to my troops. It didn't matter if I had one or a van full of recruits; he had a word of encouragement for each one and an eye-opening story from his time in the Army. He would get going on one of his war stories, and we all gave him our full attention.

Besides the fact that Scottie ran a business, he also worked part-time for Homeland Security. They hired Scottie to try and get by airport security in Atlanta. Since he was in a wheelchair, they thought just maybe security at the airport would fail to pay as much attention when he went through the gate. He developed a weapon that could be disassembled so the parts of the weapon would blend with the color of his wheelchair. It worked. When he passed through the security gate, no one noticed the extra parts on the wheelchair. When he arrived at the waiting area, Scottie began to reassemble his weapon. In short order he was surrounded by armed guards and policemen.

A year after I first met Scottie, he told me he had cancer and the prognosis was that he had six months to live. Six months later, one of the waitresses told me he had not been in since Christmas. She said he hadn't looked very good then, though he was in good spirits, as usual. I called several times, but none of my calls were answered. I suspected the worst. Then—*good news*—Scottie called. The reason I hadn't heard was that he was recovering from a bout with double pneumonia. My fears were calmed. We talked for an hour and forty-five minutes. He kept me laughing with his stories. It was hard to realize the man was in the last year of his life. But who knows who is in the last year of life? No one is promised tomorrow.

Scottie reminded me of Bob, another close friend of mine. In fact, Bob was about the same size as Scottie. He and his wife Trish had moved into a new million-dollar house on the lake a couple of months before Bob was diagnosed with liver cancer. He was given six months to live, just like Scottie. When Bob told me he had only six months to live, I asked him if there was anything I could do for him. He said, "You can come to my funeral; it's going to be a hoot!"

I'll never forget that as long as I live. I learned so much from these two men and their faith in God! I got very close to Bob in the last months of his life. In the last twenty-four hours of his life, I got to hold his hand and pray with him. He was highly medicated, but his last words to me were, "Thank you, my friend." He died the next day.

I know I went off course with my story, but I felt it was important to give a little peek into the lives of two men who looked death in the face and caused me to pause and look at life and death in a different way.

I'm Only Thirty-Nine Years Old!

The upper age limit for admission into the army is thirty-nine. Occasionally, a recruit I transported had reached that limit. The nickname the Army gave these guys was grandpa. Charlie didn't look like a grandfather. His arms were twice the size of mine, and you could tell he worked out.

I got to know Charlie pretty well on the trip down to Fort Jackson from Knoxville. He had a great personality, and he took the age jokes well. When we settled down to eat our meal, I asked him, "How are you going to keep up with these young bucks?" He said, "No problem. I can do fifty pushups in forty seconds!"

One of the recruits brought out a stopwatch, so without further ado, Charlie got down on the floor, where we had the back room to ourselves. He called out, "Give me fifty now!" What a sight! Here was an old man, by Army standards, pumping out pushups more than one every second.

The recruit with the stopwatch was giving the final countdown of four, three, two, one, as Charlie counted them up himself forty-seven, forty-eight, forty-nine, fifty. Charlie came up from the floor and hadn't even broken a sweat. The group gave him a standing ovation, and for the rest of the trip no one, including me, called him grandpa!

I Want To Get My Money's Worth!

Here's another Marine recruit story. Barry was the smallest in a group of ten going to Parris Island. He was the van clown on the trip. When the waitress asked for our orders, Barry was the first to speak. "I want to get my money's worth," he said. "I want the stir fry dinner, a steak dinner, and a hamburger platter!"

All eyes were on him, and he grinned. When his meals arrived he started on the feast before him. After twenty-five minutes, he was down to the hamburger platter. He took one bite and told the waitress. "This hamburger is too rare for me!" The waitress said, "I'll bring you another one." Without missing a beat, Barry rubbed his stomach and said, "Nah, just bring me a hot fudge sundae!"

Barry had his audience right where he wanted them. He placed the last bite of the hot fudge sundae in his mouth, jumped up and ran off to the restroom. Later we found out that all or most of his sixteen dollars worth of food, courtesy of the American taxpayer, got flushed down the toilet.

Kim's Story

Not all the stories at Shoney's were about my troops. Kim was a waitress who had waited on us for more than year. My troops and I arrived at Shoney's expecting to see Kim who usually waited on us. She had been distracted recently and hadn't seemed to be her usual self. Instead of meeting Kim, though, another waitress, Jessica, asked if we'd heard about Kim. When I said no, she proceeded to tell the story.

Kim had been depressed over the death of her mother, her father's illness and her teenager with problems, and she had turned to alcohol as a way to deal with it. She had been driving under the influence when her car left the road and hit a stone statue. It had been a bad wreck, and Kim was in the hospital in serious condition, with back and neck injuries.

Weeks turned into months. Each time we stopped at Shoney's we received updates about Kim's situation as she recuperated from the accident. Just as springtime brings new life to things that seem to be dead, God allowed Kim to have a second chance at life. After months and months of what must have been difficult rehabilitation, Kim came back to work.

The instant she approached, her smiling face told me something was different about her. I told her she seemed like a different person. She said, "Yes Terry. I've turned my life around and allowed God to come back in my life." The next thing I knew we were giving one another a hug. It was a time of joyful tears.

As Kim told her story, she had hit a statue of Jesus and the Virgin Mary. Although she remembers nothing about it, there are pictures of the statue of Jesus lying on his back with his arms in the air. And if that wasn't enough the statue of Mary was lying in Kim's lap!

I asked Kim if I could tell her story in my book and she said, "Yes, you may. You can tell my story to anyone you wish." What a joy it was to see her life turn around for God, but it was sad it took a near-death experience.

As is apparent from these few accounts, Shoney's at exit 113, just outside Columbia, South Carolina, on the way to Fort Jackson or Parris Island provided more for us than good food. I want to thank the owners of Shoney's, the managers, and all the servers, cooks, waiters, and waitresses for the service and respect they gave to my troops.

CHAPTER 16

MY LAST TRIP TO FORT KNOX

At the end of 2010, Executive Sedan and Limo lost their contract to transport recruits. After hundreds of trips, adding up to many thousands of miles, an association that had been a special privilege came to an end. The honor of making the final trip to Fort Knox, on December 29, 2009, fell to me.

I picked up Patrick and Joshua at MEPS, and we headed to Fort Knox. When I told them they were the last soldiers I'd be taking to Fort Knox and that I was writing the book about my trips, Patrick said, "Since this is your last trip, you must put us in your book." Those two young fellows and I had a great trip with a lot of good conversation.

As usual we stopped to eat at Cracker Barrel, not only for their last meal before they went into the Army but also my last meal on the way to Fort Knox. Because of the holidays, I hadn't been there in about a month. As I walked into the dining room, Cheri, who had been serving us for the past six months, greeted us and asked where I'd been. I told her I had some bad news, this was the last trip where I'd be eating at Cracker Barrel. She seemed genuinely upset by the news. As the meal progressed, Cheri stopped by our table occasionally to talk about how she was not happy about the news. "You've been my favorite person I've ever waited on. I'm going to miss you!" She was crying.

When Cheri was not working, Elaine would be my waitress. Of course, I'd found out she was a born-again Christian. She always asked my troops their names and whether they had any children. She wrote each name down on her pad, and told them that she would pray for their safety.

After we finished our meal and were ready to leave, Cheri and Elaine came over to our table to exchange telephone numbers and hugs. Elaine said she wanted me to come and speak at her church after my book was published.

As we arrived at the reception center, I said a prayer for Joshua and Patrick. As usual, I told them they needed to go to chapel every Sunday and promised it would help them get through the rest of the week and all through basic training. Then I drove away, looking in the rear view mirror, as the last images of Fort Knox faded away.

Three weeks later I received a letter from Patrick. He said, "I went to chapel just like you told me to. I fell down on my knees and started worshiping God. I'm ready to let God back in my life!" On that note, I am closing this chapter of my book, just as another chapter of my life!

God Is Good All The Time. All The, Time God Is Good!

CHAPTER 17

CONNIE

Connie Elaine Susong is my wife. When I told her I was going to write a chapter in my book about her she said, "Just a mention would be fine!" *Are you kidding me?* How in the world could I just mention in passing a person who has done nothing but give me 100% support in my adventure while writing this book? I could do what a lot of people do at the beginning of their books and say, "I want to thank my wife for all her support and loving kindness and understanding during the time I've spent writing this book!"

I could say all of that and more, but Connie has been with me every step of the way. She even rode along with me sometimes on the nine hundred mile round trips to Parris Island and she has spent hours on the cell phone, keeping me company while I drove home, bone weary. She has prayed for me while I was on the road and thanked God for bringing me home safely.

Connie loved riding along on these trips. If I'd had a rough week and driven three days in a row it was very hard on my body. That meant I had driven over 2000 miles in one week. So on those days, she would try to ride with me, and on the way home she would rub my back and neck while I drove.

On trips to Fort Jackson and Parris Island I would drive on I-40 through The Great Smoky Mountains. In the springtime the trees were waking out of their winter sleep and changing into their fresh green covering, a truly lovely sight. However, it doesn't compare to the beauty of the explosion of bright colors a few months later with the changing of the fall leaves. People drive for hundreds of miles from all over the country just to see the views I got to see several times a month—and I got paid for it. *What a great job God gave me!*

One night, after returning from a trip, I was telling Connie how pretty the leaves were and how they were almost at their peak colors. She told me she missed the change of seasons and said she'd love to ride along on my next trip. A couple of days later I got the call and she was excited to get to go. It was an awesome day, with bright sun and fresh air. Everyone on board the van was enjoying God's beauty in all the vivid colors! Everyone, that is, except Connie! She was fast asleep! I shook her and told her to wake up. I asked her, "Why did you come with me this time?" Her eyes popped opened and she said, "Oh, wow! The trees are so pretty!" I guess she needed the sleep more than the beauty, but she definitely got some beauty sleep on that trip.

Connie went with me to Parris Island only a couple of times because it was such a long trip. She loved talking to the recruits and she got to see the make-up of my job. All went smoothly the first time until we pulled up to the famous Parris Island yellow footprints. Normally, I had to go inside to let the drill instructor know we'd arrived. That would have given me a chance to warn him the woman in the front seat belonged to me and should be left alone. Unfortunately, that wasn't the way it happened.

It was dark and foggy, and the drill instructor was already outside finishing up with another group. He turned and headed our way, a big burly man who looked like Clint Eastwood in the movie *Heartbreak Ridge.* He stepped right up to the van and opened the passenger door where Connie was seated. He was in her face with his mouth already open to shout at her, as they always did, "Get out of this van and get on my yellow footprints!" I barely had time to say, "She's with me!" Connie wasn't intimidated. She just looked at him and said, "You don't want a grandma soldier like me! All I can do is bake cookies!" He just lost it, laughing out loud as he went to the side door of the van and barked out his orders to those poor new recruits, "Get out of this van and get on my yellow footprints, *now!*"

As soon as everyone was out, he came back to close Connie's door. He put his head inside the van and with a normal voice, a laugh, and a big smile he said, "You folks have a safe drive home!" Connie and I laughed all night about it.

Most of the times she rode with me were great. Before she started riding with me, I had just one request for her. Please don't embarrass me in front of my troops. I must say she fulfilled that request. She sure does a lot—well, everything—for me. I wonder if she knows how much I appreciate her support? Or did I mention that already?

CHAPTER 18

YOU'RE NOT VERY GOOD AT
THIS KILLING GAME

It was Sean's first day in the Army, and he had been waiting at MEPS for his ride to Fort Knox, Kentucky since 6:30 a.m. Since he was my only passenger, I looked forward to having a good conversation.

Sean was a great big guy but he managed to get his six feet three inch frame into the van with no trouble. Right away, I noticed he had a large cross tattoo on his left arm. He stuck his arm out so I could get a better look and began telling his touching story. His voice quivered as he told how he got the tattoo in remembrance of his best friend, Jim, who had died in a fight over a dog.

I kept listening as he went on to tell how he used to go to church every Sunday. "I was trying to do everything the right way in the eyes of God," he said. "Then I got mad at God for taking my best friend away. He was only fourteen. I started taking cocaine and shooting up heroin. I turned my back on God and my life started down a slippery slope."

I continued to listen as he told about his mother and father, who were both heavy drinkers and also into drugs. After a period of time his mother divorced his father. Things didn't get any better because she married a man who also did drugs and drank, as he put it, like a fish. One day his new stepfather came in from work and, as usual, had been drinking.

Sean told me, "I just couldn't take it anymore! I body slammed him into the large entertainment center and tried my best to kill him! My aunt and uncle both had to pull me off of him." Then he said, "About a month later we got into another fist fight, and I tried to kill him again. This time he ran away from me before I could get my knife."

"Wow, Sean!" I said. "You're not very good at this killing game are you?" He just laughed.

"Wait a minute! You haven't heard the best story, yet!" I kept listening.

"John, my stepfather, came in drunk again, and I could tell he was wasted. He yelled at me to fix him a drink. So, I went in the kitchen and fixed him his drink. This time I decided he needed a little extra punch in his punch. I reached under the sink and got a box of rat poison and mixed it in the drink."

My heart sank. "Oh, my God, Sean! What happened? Did he die?"

Sean said, "Well, after consuming the drink he started to hold his stomach, and he was having difficulty breathing. My next step was to go outside and dig his grave. When I went back inside to check on him he was on the floor holding his stomach, and his eyes were rolling back in his head."

At that moment his mother came home. When she saw John in the condition he was in, she screamed, "What's wrong with him?" Sean said he told her, "Oh, he'll be dead soon. I gave him a drink of whiskey and rat poison." Sean told me she was concerned that if he died she'd take the blame, since he had abused both of them.

It was hard for me to pay attention to my driving. I wanted to pull over and just listen to the rest of his drama, but I kept driving and listening.

Sean went on with the saga. "Well, John had so much alcohol and drugs in his system that it absorbed the rat poison. He threw up the special cocktail that I'd made for him. He recovered after about an hour, not knowing that I had tried to kill him."

"Wow, Sean! You're not very good at this killing game, are you?" I said again. Sean just laughed. I asked him, "Sean, can you see that God has been working in your life and you didn't even know it? You have tried to kill your stepfather three times without any success. Had you been able to kill him any one of those times, you wouldn't be on your way to the Army. You'd be sitting in a prison cell."

Sean seemed to get a lot out of our conversation. I could feel trust building between us. He talked more about wanting to turn his life around. He said the Army was to be his new lease on life. I told him what God had done in my life and how I knew what it was like to be away from home. I also told him that without Jesus in my life, I would never have made it through basic training and a year in Vietnam. Sean was the one listening to every word I said then. *I prayed God would give me the right words.*

We went through the gate at Fort Knox. Something inside me told me now was the time to reach this young man. I pulled over to the side of the road and asked Sean if I could say a prayer for him. He said yes, and I prayed for him as I have for all of my troops. *God please bring Sean home safe and sound.* Then I asked Sean if he would like to get everything right with God before we parted. He said he would.

Sean asked Jesus to come into his heart and to forgive him of his sins. *God bless you, Sean! You are now in God's hands.*

CHAPTER 19

MY FINAL WORDS

The two hardest things about writing a book are finding a starting place and finding a place to stop. It has been three years since I took that first trip to Parris Island with Tony. In those three years, I transported several hundred young men and women from MEPS the short trip to the Knoxville airport. Instead of a ride in a van to basic training with me, they took an airplane to their destination. I showed them the same love and respect I gave to those who rode all the way to basic training with me. However, the results were not the same, since there was no opportunity to give them cards or to build any kind of relationship. I regret sending all those young folks on their way without a prayer and a promise to write.

After the Fort Knox run was over, I never knew how much longer I would continue to drive to Fort Jackson and Parris Island. As long as the good Lord gave me health and the desire to continue, I knew I'd take on this job as a badge of honor.

My main focus was on the troops. During the five to eight hours I spent with them, we could build a close relationship, one that made possible the many interactions that called forth from them the inspiring letters I've received.

Looking back, I'd have to say my troops fell into three categories:

1) The Shy (those who wouldn't say *Boo* to me)
2) The Crybaby (those said *Boo-Hoo*, crying or near crying about leaving their loved ones), and
3) The Overexcited (those who said a loud *Ya-Hoo*!).

During the first six months of my driving I didn't say the prayer, nor did I have any cards to give them. I had no intention of writing a spiritual or inspirational book. I was going to write just about the funny things that happened on the last day of freedom for the recruits I transported. Then, on my way home one night, my thoughts running amok as they do quite often while driving, a flash came to me. I suddenly knew that I needed to say a prayer for my troops before dropping them off. I could not get that thought off my mind. Finally, I made the decision to start praying at the end of the next trip, which was to be for Parris Island.

We had a good trip with everyone in a good mood but I was a little nervous. I pulled into the small area that would become my regular prayer zone. I asked whether anyone cared if I prayed. Since this was my first prayer, I was a little concerned I might get a negative response. It was a great relief when I heard the loud response, "Please do, Sir. We need all the help that we can get!"

One night when I went to Fort Jackson, I asked for the same permission. There was no objection, so I began to pray. I was almost finished with the prayer when all of a sudden one of the women started to yell. "Let me out of here, let me out of here! The smell. The smell!" Later, I found out that she belonged to the Black Art, a group that honors witchcraft. I had been told if you pray for a Black Art group and use the name of Jesus it put an aroma around them they didn't like! At any rate, this young woman thought she was a witch and acted accordingly.

A couple of months passed and I felt that something was missing. I needed something that I could leave behind with my troops so I could get some future feedback from them. That's how my card was born. Later, I discovered I could acquire copies of the book *Psalm 91: God's Shield of Protection*, written by Peggy Joyce Ruth and Angelia Ruth Schum, for distribution to the military. I began handing out a copy of that book, along with a small cross pin.

Once I began praying and handing out cards with my name and address, I figured letters would start flowing in. It didn't happen at first. The good Lord had a different idea for me. Weeks went by without one letter. I continued to pray and hand out my cards, but I felt a little discouraged.

One Sunday morning in church the sermon said all God wants you to do is plant his seed, and let him do the watering and the harvesting. I was planting the seed and then worrying too much about whether the seed was germinating. I learned through the sermon that it was my job to be the best Christian possible, pray for them and give them a card. After that lesson, the letters started to arrive. I always answered the letters within a couple of days. Sometimes they wrote more than one letter. One person said mine was the first letter he received in basic training.

The opportunity to continue ministering to my troops through correspondence, when the driving was all over, meant a great deal to me. Now, through this little book, I've been given the opportunity to go beyond my troops, to give everyone a glimpse into one of the obscure parts of a new recruit's life. In the process, I couldn't help but reflect upon my own life.

Now that God has allowed me to live past my fifties and spill over into my sixties, I've been thinking about the cycle of my life. At twenty I was the same age as most of the troops going to basic training. From twenty to forty-eight, I worked as a career firefighter and was a tough guy, funny man, with a first class ego. Between forty-eight and sixty or so, I retired, traveled, moved from Ohio to Tennessee, ran out of money and worked at odd jobs. At sixty and a little more, I started transporting recruits, writing a book, getting a new outlook on life. *Life! It's amazing.*

At the end, the company had financial difficulties causing Connie and me a great deal of trouble of our own. It hasn't been easy for me to deal with the way the company handled their responsibilities to me. I have had to struggle mightily to balance the wonderful good of the entire enterprise with this unfortunate conclusion. I try to remind myself of what I've told my troops over and over again, it's prayer that will bring me peace—as well as thinking about the many letters telling me my ministry with the recruits made their lives better.

Now I will go on to do whatever task God sets before me. Of course, a call just *might* come, assigning me to take another run to Fort Jackson or even Parris Island. So, just in case I should find myself driving once more, and you should happen to be traveling on I-40 or I-26, and you happen to see an old, bald headed guy driving a van sporting a sign on the side that reads *Executive Sedan*—well, just toot your horn, roll down the window and holler, "Sir, when is our next stop?"

Maybe there will be a Pilot station or Cracker Barrel or a Shoney's at the next exit and we can have a cup of coffee together! May God bless you in all you do.

God Is Good All The Time. All The, Time God Is Good!

I would love to hear your thoughts about this book. My email address is terrysusong@aol.com.

APPENDIX I

A LEGEND OF THE GREAT SMOKY MOUNTAINS

Marvin "Popcorn" Sutton was a legend of the Great Smoky Mountains. He was a mountain man who made moonshine his whole life, a trade the learned from his father. When he was sixty-two years old, the Feds moved in and arrested him for the manufacturing of illegal alcohol, possessing an illegal firearm, and failure to pay taxes on the sale of his moonshine. He was sentenced to eighteen months in a Federal prison. In 1999 Popcorn wrote a book entitled *Me and My Licker*. He was also featured in a documentary on The History Channel called *Hillbilly: The Real Story*. Later, when he was diagnosed with cancer, he and was allowed to serve out his sentence at home. On March 16, 2009, Popcorn Sutton committed suicide by carbon monoxide poisoning. His funeral received national attention and was attended by country and western singing star Hank Williams, Jr.

http://www.youtube.com/watch?v=EPuWX7d7yEw

APPENDIX II

PRAYER FOR MY TROOPS

DEAR HEAVENLY FATHER

PLEASE BLESS EACH ONE OF THESE PRECIOUS SOULS.

I PRAY THAT YOU WILL ALLOW THEM TO LISTEN WITH OPEN EARS AND TO BE ON THE SAME PAGE AS THEIR INSTRUCTORS.

ALSO DEAR FATHER, PLEASE, PLEASE ALLOW THEM TO WRITE HOME AND CALL HOME EVERY CHANCE THEY HAVE SO THEY CAN BE ON THE SAME PAGE AS THEIR LOVED ONES BACK AT HOME.

DEAR LORD, IF THEY ARE CALLED ONTO FOREIGN SOIL, I PRAY THAT YOU WILL BUILD A HEDGE OF PROTECTION AROUND THEM AND RETURN THEM SAFELY HOME TO THEIR LOVED ONES.

AS THEY SEEK YOU, I PRAY THAT YOU WILL REACH YOUR HAND DOWN TO THEM, AND AS THEY REACH THEIR HANDS UP TO YOU, BRING THEM INTO YOUR ARMS.

AND LASTLY LORD, I ASK YOU TO PLACE YOUR HAND ON THIS VAN AND GUIDE ME SAFELY HOME, AS YOU ALWAYS DO, SO THAT I MAY RETURN AGAIN WITH MORE TROOPS.

AMEN

God Is Good All The Time. All The, Time God Is Good!

APPENDIX III

THE YELLOW FOOTPRINTS

Jim Cline (my boss at executive Sedan and Limo) was in the Marines Corp for twenty-five years. He gave me a short history of the yellow prints.

The Marine Corps is the only branch of the service using footprints. There are four rows (lefts and rights) set fifteen deep at a forty-five degree angle. When the recruits line up with their feet on the yellow footprints, the DI will have a perfect formation, and each recruit will be in perfect position. From now on, the recruits would take this position whenever addressing a Marine, sailor, or civilian during their stay at Parris Island—the first step in transforming them into Marines.

The Marines have been training male recruits since 1915 and brought on female recruits in 1949. The only other basic training site for the Marine Corps is Camp Pendleton, California. It is nicknamed Camp Hollywood. All recruits west of the Mississippi go to Camp Pendleton, and east of the Mississippi go to Parris Island. The exception is that all women entering the Marine Corps go to Parris Island, South Carolina.

APPENDIX IV

LETTERS FROM MY TROOPS

Date	Letter
11/17/2009	Dear Terry,

Thank you very much for writing back. I thought you might remember me and my crazy singing as well. To my surprise even my platoon enjoys it. When everybody had a hard day at the range I was singing on the bus and some of my platoon heard me and they have me sing sometimes when they are down.

My ankle is doing much better now, and im ready to finish up basic now. I have also went to chapel here on Sunday. I enjoy going it gives me hope to finish out my weeks and get home.

I hope your back is coming along nice. It sounds like it would be good. They taught us here slow is smooth, smooth is fast. So maybe this back is an award winner in the making.

I hate to hear about the rocks. I'm very glad no one was injured. I bet its really difficult at times with the extra miles added to your route. Hopefully they will get it cleared up soon.

Thank you for everything you have done for me and many others. I'll keep you in my prayers. If you want to see pictures of my company go to www.facebook.com/alwaysforward134. They have a lot on there well that's what i've been told. The two mates that went down on the same trip should also be on there. Oh they are doing good as well. I talk to them when time permits.

Psalms 91 is a very good book. Be safe on your trips and tell the future "troops" <u>Basic is everything you make it. It can be hard or it can be easy. But keep your head up and keep moving forward.</u>" Its almost lights out here though so ill close for now.

Always Forward,
Samantha

P.S. and tell future troops your drill sergeants just want you to be successful. Don't take anything personal.

05/03/2009   Mr. Susong,

I was just writing to say thank you for the motivational conversation and inspirational prayer from you on my way to Fort Knox. With God on my side, the training is nowhere near as bad as I expected. I'm glad my trip wasn't as military as everthing else, because it provided much needed spiritual guidance. Once again, I'd like to say thank you, and I'm sorry I didn't write you sooner. As you can imagine, my schedule's pretty busy.

God Bless You
Josh

04/02/2009   Hi Mr. Susong

Thank you for being a real nice person and for being a person to talk to. But Ion't like to write much but it passes the time and you are a generous person with a heart and tell your wife I said hi too. And I read Psalm 91 also and it has helped.

Thank you
Steven

06/29/2008   Hey Terry,

How have you been? I'm doing good but I still haven't got shipped to real basic yet. I have made a lot of new friends. I'm in Series 177 #009. A lot of the other groups don't like us because we have come together as one big team, and we do everything right. I can't wate until I get done with all this and get back home, I miss everybody all ready. Well, I have to go now I'll write you again.

PVT Aaron

08/22/2011   Dear Terry,

Thanks again for the ride to Parris Island. It has been a challenging experience so far but I'm having a problem. I wrote my family over a week ago and haven't gotten any reply. If you can contact them I would appreciate it very much, thank you.

James
Connie
Vickie

Dear James,

Thank you for the letter. I called your mother as requested. She stated that everything is working out for you now. I am so happy for you. I know how much mail call means to a soldier in basic training. You feel so good when your name is called, and so bad when it is not. I hope that you will continue to write to me and I will always answer your letter.

If there is anything else that I can do for you please let me know. Your mother told me that you are enjoying the Psalm 91 book. This book will help you in more ways than you will ever know if you put to practice the knowledge that it offers.

I hope that things are getting better for you as each week passes. Just keep up your faith in God, and your prayer life and God will bless you.

I am here for you and I am looking forward to your next letter.

From the old man that took you to basic training.
Terry Susong

P.S. MAY GOD BLESS YOU AND KEEP YOU AND MAY HIS FACE SHINE UPON YOU AND GIVE YOU PEACE. AMEN

07/12/2008   Hey Terry,

Sorry I haven't wrote you in a while I've kinda been busy. So how have you been doing? I've been OK. Training is hard on some days but other days aren't so bad. We have done a lot of fun stuff so far. We are about to start hand to hand combat and do the gas chamber. I think that's going to be great fun. I have made a lot of friends since basic has started. I got to beat one of them up in pugils, he didn't have a chance. My drill sergeants are rally laid back and cool about things but they really work us out a lot. They even let us buy cameras so we can take pictures of all our new friends. They give us extra time on the phones and all kinds of things that the other platoons don't get to do. I really can't wait for basic to end so I can get back to my family back home. I really miss them. It's hard not being able to see my lil sister but I'll keep pushing forward and hang in here and everything will be OK. Well Terry I have to get ready for fire guard or CQ or something like that and I still need to shower.

Write me when you get a chance.
PVT Aaron

07/20/2008   Dear Aaron,

Thank you for the great Letter. It is very good to hear from you and I am glad that basic training has started for you. It sounds like you are having a very good start. I pray God will continue to bless you daily. I know that basic training can be tuff at times but I also know that it can be rewarding also. Your letter gave me a lift for the day. Tomorrow I will be going to Paris Island with a bunch of JARHEADS. Last week I had 15!

I just got back from New York City on vacation. We took our grandson to see Yankee Stadium before they tear it down at the end of the season. What a fun trip! I know that I do not want to live in New York City! What a rat race with all the subways and buses and traffic. It was great to get back home.

Are you going to chapel every Sunday? This will help you in your daily walk with God and it will also help you in your daily grind. I am anxious to hear about how God is working in your life. Please write me back and share with me some of your highlights of your new life. You will never know how much our trip to Fort Knox has effected my life in a positive way. Our talks on the way was very enlighting to me and I hope that it helped you to talk to me. I will never forget it! The Book of John in the Old Testament is a great place to start your reading of the Bible.

Aaron, I will be praying for you. If there is anything that I can do for you please just ask and I will do everything in my power to make it happen.

God Is Good All The Time. All The, Time God Is Good!

Your new friend in Christ,
Terry Susong

05/22/2011   Mr. Susong

I don't know if you remember me but my name is Robert, you dropped me off at Fort Jackson SC on April 12th. I just wanted to thank you for a few things. The first thing is simple bringing me here, it was the best choice I have ever made. At first things were rough and now the days are just flying by. Graduation is the 23rd of June, so I've got about a month left. Second is praying for me before you dropped me off, that meant a lot. It made me think about everything. I am just about done with that book. It is a good one. I am going to order a bunch and hand them out once I get home. Every night before I go to bed I say this verse.

Corinthians, Ch 4, Verse 8,9,10

8 We are hard pressed on every side, yet not crushed; we are perplexed, but not in despair

9 Persecuted, but not forsaken; struck down but not destroyed

10 Always carrying about in the body the dying of the Lord Jesus, that the life of Jesus also may be manifested in our body.

This keeps me strong and I'm sure it would keep other young soldiers strong as well. So I ask if you could read this to just a few of the soldiers you transport. Thank you Mr. Susong.

Robert

10/18/2010   Hey Mr. Susong

It's Joe you brought me to Fort Jackson on Sept 23 and it was me and you. Thanks for everything that you told me. I just got my phase change today from red to white. I have the nicest and coolest drill sargants ever. They treat us good. I like it here I'm gonna make it here doing (DRM) "Basic Rifle Marksmanship." I've been wrighting my mom and dad a lot. How have you been I've got in a good platoon We all pretty good I've got a bunch of friends Esp the ones in our squad and in my bunch like now we got like 7 people in here just talking it up. But all in all I just wanted to say thank you for your kindness and hospitally.

Pvt. Joseph

01/20/2009   Hello,

I don't know if you remember me, but you dropped me and 6 other guys out at Ft Knox Jan 5 O the 7. 3 of us wound up in the same platoon. We are in our 2nd week of BCT and 2 of us are doing fine. Terry, the one that was group leader has been in a little trouble and has had 2 article 15's slapped on him.

I just wanted to say thank you for being so kind to us on the trip up here.

Tyler

09/22/2010   Mr. Susong,

I'm glad you remember me. I'm almost through with basic only 2 more weeks. Next week we go to Victory Forge and tomorrow is the final Pt test. Hope I pass it. Everything else is good except for drama in the female bay and platoon. We were called individuals for awhile because nobody seemed to work together. Sometimes we do good. I liked that 1st chapter of your book. Is it out yet? Can't wait to be able to read the whole book. I'm trying to stay positive and most of all believe and that I can do it. This is a quick letter because we have studying to do for IN4 it's inspection I think. Something like that. Also I'm trying to be calm about the Pt test. I have stressed about Pt many times. All I'm thinking is that tomorrow is the big day. I don't know what else to say or write. I'll let you know how I did. God bless you!

Mayra

09/25/2010   Terry,

Hello again my friend. I finished the book and each morning I have made it a habit to read Psalms 91 before beginning my day. I truly have noticed a difference in my life. I passed my P.T. test 2 days ago, and I believe it was all thru prayer. My battle did fail but we are all working with her. So she can retake on family day morning. I liked the chapter you sent me, and will be waiting for the book so I can read it all. I managed to hurt my hip during P.T. test though so I ask that you keep me in your prpayers that the bone scan results come back okay so that I will be able to make up the 10 mile march that I will be missing come Monday. Have a wonderful day & God Bless!

Your Troop,
Amanda

09/11/2011   Dear Terry,

Sorry I haven't responded sooner. We've been so so busy that I've barely had time to write my family. To be honest I've not read any of your book yet, but I do plan to at AIT. I'll have a lot more free time there to do as I please.

It's sad to reflect back on this day 10 years ago. I was in the 8th grade, most of the others here were in 4th grade. I remember watching it all on TV that day. We had a concert last night by a country singer named Kelly Pickler. I've never heard of her before but she was pretty good.

As for business here, the 28th is family day and the 29th is graduation. I'm so ecstatic to be near the end. We have one more full week of training then we have Victory Forge (a 4 day field training event) and we're done, except for outprocessing. After Ft Jackson it's on to Monterrey, California for me for 1 year of AIT. They're going to teach me a language that's why it's so long.

Anyways, I hope everything is going well for you and you have had more interesting people. I will write you from AIT though I'm not scheduled to start it until Oct 31. I'm not sure if it'll actually work that way though.

Sincerely—The Agnostic
Shawn

12/18/2010   CHRISTMAS CARD with photos

Terry,

I hope you have a great Christmas! I figured I would write and let you know everything is great here. I got stationed back on Parris Island go figure. Well enjoy the Holidays with your family

Jessica

07/20/2009   Mr. Susong

How is everything on the outside? This is PV2, James; you brought me and one other person to Fort Knox from Knoxville on May 5th. Things are going good here. We have just finished the basic training portion, and had family weekend. It really helped out to see my family. We have started our AIT section now, and we are on the tanks. Finally. I am excited about what is going on now. Everything has calmed down a lot as well which is good. It won't be long till we are out of here though, August 28 is graduation. So how are you and your wife doing with Mona-Vie[?]. Hope it has been working out well. Well keep having safe trips taking trainees to basic.

Take Care
James

10/29/2009   Mr. Susong,

Hello. I don't know if you remember me or not. But I rode up to Fort Knox with you on the 21st of July from the Knoxville MEPS. I just now found your card and had some free time. So I decided to write this letter. Right now I am in the AIT portion of my Cavalry Scout OSET training. I have 3 weeks to go. I must say the bible verse on your card helped motivate me to get this far so for that I thank you. Well that's all I can think of for now. Write back if you want to.

Sincerely,
Travis

11/21/2009   Terry,

I know it has been a long while since our bus ride up to Fort Knox on 19oct, but I wanted to write and let you know that the 5 of us have all been doing really well and pushing through. We all ended up in the same Company, but in different platoons; Andrew is in 1st platoon, Haberle and Hurd is in 2nd, I am in 3rd and Willie is in 4th platoon. I had a rough time at first, home sick and lonely but I reconnected with the guys from our ride up and things have gotten a lot better.

We spent about 4-1/2 days in reception and now have spent about 4 weeks in basic. We have done a lot of training and a lot of PT. As we go farther through this I find it is fun and getting easier by the day. Hurd has gained a lot of confidence and I can see it in the way he carries himself. I am glad that he has Haberle with him to encourage him.

So we have hit all the obstacle courses, the WBC chamber, Land nav[?], combatives, a lot of classes, BRM, a road march, and all that PT. We have gotten a lot stronger and faster, smarter and more military minded.

I wanted to thank you for the encouragement on the ride, and the prayers that I am sure we are receiving. They have all been helping I feel really good about this. We have 25 days till exodus. It will be great to have these 2 weeks away from Drill Sergeants and young stupid privates that can't stop talking at attention. At any rate thank you again for the great ride up, the emotional support and the prayers.

PVT Kremsreiter

PS If you would, please send the title of your book so I can look for it.

10/23/2009   Dear Mr. Susong,

Hello, you drove me and two other soldiers to Fort Jackson SC on Sept 30th. I wanted to thank you for doing that. That day I was really nervous and didn't think I could do this. But I'm still going strong. I did get hurt though. I think everything will be OK though. I think the hard part is being away from my family. I miss them all so much. I love getting letters they keep me going from day to day.

I remember you saying something about writing a book. Are you still doing it? If so I would like to have a copy of it.

The other soldiers that rode in the van seem to be doing good. I see them from time to time. It was really fast pace here at first but now I think I'm getting used to the way things work around here.

Mr. Susong I have a favor to ask you. Could you please pray for me? So that I can graduate and go home to my family also that my ankles get better.

Thank you for all you did for me. I hope to hear from you soon.

My address is: [shown elsewhere]

*Make sure you write "3rd" on the back of the envelope.

Thank you.

11/13/2009   Dear Terry,

Hi, it's Brittany, you brought me to Ft Jackson about 2 weeks ago. I was in the group that had the Wichen if you remember. I sat in the front seat. I'm doing OK, everyday I stay gives me a little more confidence that I can actually make it. I am looking foreward to Christmas exodus and spending time with my husband and family. Each day we get busier and busier, and I have very little time to study my Bible. I'm also dying to eat some junk food. Well, I need to go, time for formation.

Pray for Me,
Brittany

PS Please write me and tell me how my beautiful Appalachian Mountains are fairing this winter.

09/16/2009   Hello Terry!

Tim again, I received your letter some time back but this is the first real chance I have had to write you back. Right now I am sitting in sick quarters, however, I am all right I do have a severe URI that required I be put in quarters for a few days . . . Thank you for your letter, and honestly, thank you for your concern & prayers. It is quite rare to meet anyone who honestly and truly cares . . . Its my pleasure to have run across paths with you! I did read Psalm 91, I have read it before but when I reflected on it, that is almost the perfect Psalm for a soldier~ As for basic, everything here is going over very smoothly (other than being sick). Like before the main concern is my children . . . I do miss them very much! My wife as well, but in the end this is the reason I am here, for my kids, for my wife . . .

Well for now I need to get a little more rest! But, thank you again! I really would like a copy of your book when you get it finished too! Regardless of how things end up I feel I am a better man for this & in eternity & new friend. This life is simply the shadow land of things to come.

As always
All good things

Your friend
Tim

08/02/2009   Dear Mr. Susong,

I mean to write to you sooner, but I have been extremely busy. I wanted to say thank you for a fun trip up here. A couple of the guys that rode up here in the van are in my company. A few others went to Bravo. I think I've had an interesting experience here so far. I sprained my ankle early on into it, but I'm back to training full force. I didn't miss any mandatory training though. So I'm still on track to graduating on Sept 11th. We spent all week last week at the firing range. We were grouping and zeroing our weapons. I had range detail so I had MRES for breakfast & lunch 4 days in a row. I finally got pancakes this morning. It's funny how the little things excite me now. My platoon is full of the people who don't want to be a team & keep getting us in trouble. I hope they grow out of that soon. We're starting week 5 now, so it shouldn't take them too long. I go to church every Sunday here. It's a big stress reliever & nice to hear someone preaching His word instead of hearing "front leaning rest position move" all day. My platoon's (4th) drill sergeants are great though. They actually act line we're human & not just dumb privates. I miss my cell phone though. Last time I checked I had about 15 voicemails that I haven't gotten to listen to yet. I'm hoping we get phone calls again soon. Well, I better get going. We have formation soon & I have to get ready. Say a prayer for me. I need it. And can you please pray for all my battle buddies too? Thanks again.

I miss being able to change the radio stations in the van. The front seat was the best.

Sincerely,
Stefanie

04/10/2011   Dear Terry,

Hello, this is Jeremy "Brandon". I hope you remember me. You dropped me off at Ft Knox in March. I was the person who had my mother pass away 3 days before I met you. You also gave me a book called "Psalm 91 God's Shield of Protection." I wanted to thank you for that book and tell you that it has helped out a lot. I read it all the time. I have battle buddies that I share it with also.

Anyways I wanted to let you know that I am doing OK. I have had a lot of fun so far. There are some really good people here that I have become friends with. they help me with dealing with my mom's death. Most people said basic training would be hard, but it is what you make of it. I find it very interesting and fun. There are hard times, but there are hard times in anything you do. I would like to thank you again, and I hope you are well. If you would like to write back, you are most welcome. I have been praying for you and everyone back home in Tennessee. Take care of yourself and your family.

Sincerely,
Brandon

11/26/2009   Dear Terry,

        "Dude" lol

<u>Happy Thanksgiving!</u>

We have one drill sergeant watching all 300 of us in Charlie Company. Some more drill sergeants are coming in a bit and they are serving us lunch.

Thanksgiving lunch was great! We were served by our drill sergeants, and officers! I was nervous, but sat down and enjoyed my thanksgiving with my new family! We had soo much food and ice cream and eggnog and cheesecake! Oh, yeah candy! lol

Everyone was happy! Then we got to call home for the rest of the day! It was great! I called my husband three times and we talked about working out our problems and staying together. I told him that he has to change or I won't stay with him. So, this Christmas will make us or brake us!

11/27/2009

Hey we have been doing detail all day b/c one stupid female that is leaving in two weeks drop her phone in a bag of water and she went to the D.S. and said we did it and stole her other phone! Well, we had to take all our stuff out of our lockers and come to find out she had her phone!

I hate all this crap! I came here to be a soldier not to be stuck in a boxing ring! lol

12/06/2009

What's up?

Did you get my last letter? I'm thinking about going to church today. I believe in God but I'm not as close to him as I used to be but it's fine.

So, did you and your wife have a good thanksgiving? Mine was good had a lot of food.

It's been stressful and hard lately, trying to overcome my thoughts and mind. I shot 26 out of 40 it's passing but I want to do better. My biggest problem is my helmet and vest are too big and I can't see in the prone position, on belly.

10 more days and I get to go home for Christmas! I can't wait to see my son! His daddy wants to work it out with me so we are trying more now. I love him I just want him to be more romantic and out going. OK I'll see this brake.

After Christmas I only have 4 more weeks here and then 6 weeks at AIT! Can't wait to get it over with its so cold! lol

Oh well it makes me stronger. We are at war still and I'm a bit afraid b/c I know we are going after AIT. I'm trying to get my husband squared away so if I do die than he will be fine and my son will have money. I hope I don't die but I'm getting ready for it.

Well, take care
Forty Rounds
~~~~~~~~~

05/04/2009   Dear Terry

    I hope you remember me. My name is Timmy. We had a conversation about God on the way to Fort Knox. You took me and another guy named Smith. I read that Psalm 91 all the time. It gives me a lot of hope in all that I'm going through. Anyway I'm doing good. I'm a little banged up, but I will be OK. I wanna thank you for all your prayers and for praying for me before you dropped us off. It's no mistake that God puts people like you in my way to be a blessing here on earth, and for that I'm thankful too. Sometimes we are the only Jesus some people will probably ever see here on earth. I told you a little about my girlfriend K.C. Hicks that is also in the National Guard and about where she will be going. Anyway you told me to give you the date when she will be leaving for her Basic so maybe you could set it up to drive her and others to Fort Jackson. Well her ship date is May 19th and I want you to try to take her if you can. I wanna send you a short letter and some money for a rose to give her to let her know how much I appreciate her. If you can pull this off that would be great. If not don't stress about it.

Dustin wrote to me, "I have read *Psalm 91* at least five or six times. Each time that I read it, I received the help that I needed for the rest of the day. Will you please send me so more Bible verses to help me?"

Samantha wrote, "Mr. Susong I have a favor to ask you. Would you please pray for me, so that I can go home to my family and also that my ankles will fill better?

Alexandria wrote, "Mr. Susong . . . How are you? I am sure you don't remember me, but I rode in your van to Fort Jackson from the Knoxville MEPS on January 20th for basic training. I was looking through my address envelope and I found the card that you gave me. I bought a Bible at the PX today so I could "Check out . . . *Psalm 91*. But I waited until the lights out to read it, which was about two minutes ago. I found it very comforting and inspirational, and I'm very glad that I didn't throw your card away!"

Joshua wrote, "Dear Terry . . . Hey, I'm not sure if you remember me, but you changed my life and I want start off by saying 'thank you'. You drove me to Fort Jackson for basic training on the 23rd of May. On that day you introduced me to God. You gave me your card and told me to write to you. I'm just sorry that it has taken so long to send you a letter. I would have written sooner but I left your card in my Bible and I found it today when I was reading it. I wrote to my girlfriend and she was very happy when I told her that I got saved and was going to church and reading my Bible every chance I got. Her parents were also proud of me. I thank you the most for telling me that I did not have to wait until I got back home to get saved. You also helped me make the most important step in my life: my faith for God has helped me stay motivated and has helped me keep strong through the tougher times here. Thank you for everything."

Edwards Brothers Malloy
Oxnard, CA USA
July 25, 2014